CAROLE BUCK

RED-HOT SATIN

SILHOUETTE *Desire*®

Published by Silhouette Books New York

America's Publisher of Contemporary Romance

SILHOUETTE BOOKS
300 East 42nd St., New York, N.Y. 10017

RED-HOT SATIN

ISBN: 0-373-05677-X

First Silhouette Books printing November 1991

Printed in the U.S.A.

Books by Carole Buck

Silhouette Desire

Time Enough for Love #565
Paradise Remembered #614
White Lace Promises #644
Red-Hot Satin #677

Silhouette Romance

Make-believe Marriage #752

CAROLE BUCK

is a television news writer and movie reviewer who lives in Atlanta. She is single. Her hobbies include cake decorating, ballet and traveling. She collects frogs, but does not kiss them. Carole says she's in love with life; she hopes the books she writes reflects this.

Prologue

Hayley Jerome glared at the readout on her computer monitor. Oh, no, she thought, shaking her head in frustration. Not again!

She felt her tortoiseshell-rimmed glasses start to slide down her nose. She shoved them back into place with a quick poke and continued studying the data before her.

Hayley had spent much of the past three weeks trying to trace the paper trail of one of the slickest money laundering schemes she'd ever seen. She'd felt certain she was close to penetrating the core of the illegal operation. But instead of finally striking pay dirt, she'd just discovered she'd been led down another blind alley into yet another dummy corporation.

Patience, she counseled, tapping a sequence of keys and clearing the screen. Slow and steady wins the race.

The phone on the corner of Hayley's desk shrilled suddenly. She picked it up after the second ring.

"Extension 2976," she announced.

Silence.

"Extension 2976," she repeated crisply.

"Hayley?" a distinctive feminine voice inquired.

Hayley caught her breath. "Mother?"

"Oh, it *is* you," Pamela Delaney Jerome Martinez de la Madrid Touissante Pynchley-Smythe Horowitz said with a delighted laugh. "I wasn't certain. You sounded so... so professional."

"The Justice Department encourages that in its employees," Hayley returned dryly.

"I'm sure it does, dear," her mother agreed. "And you're absolutely wonderful at it." She laughed again, then continued, "Now, I know it's naughty of me to call you at your office. I was going to phone your apartment, but I was afraid I'd have to deal with your answering machine, and you know how I feel about that. I haven't gotten you at a bad time, have I?"

Hayley glanced at the computer screen and suppressed a sigh. "No, Mother."

"You're sure? I know how you try to spare my feelings when I call at an inopportune moment."

"Mother—"

"Remember when you were at college in Boston and I was married to Sir Percy and living in Hong Kong? I never could figure out the time difference, you know. I tried, but I always ended up phoning you in the dead of night or at the crack of dawn. Of course, you never complained. And every time I asked if I'd woken you up, you lied and said no. It was so sweet of you. But I want you to tell me the truth now. If this isn't a good time—"

"This is a *fine* time," Hayley interrupted firmly. "You couldn't have picked a better moment to call me if you'd tried. So, what can I do for you?"

There was a brief silence on the other end. Then, "Why, nothing, dear. But it's kind of you to offer."

Hayley struggled with an escalating sense of exasperation. "I didn't mean it literally."

"Excuse me?"

Hayley decided it would be pointless to try to explain. "Why did you call, Mother?" she asked.

"Why did I call?" Pamela parroted, her tone suggesting she suspected this might be a trick question. "To talk to you, of course."

Of course, Hayley thought. "To talk to me about what?"

"About my surprise."

Hayley was suddenly very glad she was sitting down. The sound of her mother uttering the word "surprise" tended to make her dizzy and weak-kneed. The sound of her mother uttering the word "marriage" had the same effect. The sound of her mother uttering *both* words...

God. Hayley didn't want to think about it.

"Your...surprise?"

"Well, actually, it's *our* surprise," Pamela amended. "Elliot's and mine, I mean."

Elliot, Hayley knew, was former U.S. Representative Elliot Parker, her mother's new fiancé. Her anxiety level ratcheted up a notch or two.

"Let me guess," she said, deliberately keeping her voice light. "You and Elliot have eloped."

Dead silence on the other end.

Oh, no, Hayley thought, aghast. They have!

"Mother—" she began, feeling decidedly frayed around the edges. She'd taken an immediate liking to Elliot Parker when she'd met him the previous month in San Francisco. He'd impressed her as the kind of person who made plans and stuck to them. This made him very different from the woman he was engaged to wed. Hayley's mother—as Hayley was acutely aware—couldn't stick to a plan unless she was stapled to it. But if Elliot had agreed to run off and get married—

Pamela laughed suddenly. "Fooled you."

"Mother!"

Another laugh. "I'm sorry, dear, but I couldn't resist."

Hayley closed her eyes and prayed for strength. She adored her mother. Truly, she did. But sometimes the woman drove her right up the wall.

"You and Elliot haven't eloped, then?" she questioned, opening her eyes again. She wanted to be absolutely certain of the facts.

"No, of course not," her mother returned reassuringly. "We're still getting married in December. Elliot's got everything organized. He's a lot like you, Hayley. He makes lists. He never loses anything. He always knows exactly where he's supposed to be and what he's supposed to be doing. Your dear, dead father—my Henry—was the same way. So strong. So stable..." Pamela's commentary tailed off into a wistful sigh.

"I know," Hayley said softly, her irritation of a few moments before melting like frost in sunshine. "I know." Although she'd only been five when her father had died, her sense of what sort of man he'd been was very vivid, thanks to her mother.

There was a short silence.

"I don't think I'll ever elope again," Pamela remarked eventually. "It was fun with Jean Luc, but once is enough. I don't like to repeat myself in affairs of the heart."

Hayley decided to let this comment pass.

"So, Mother, what's your surprise?" she prompted after a moment. "And please, don't tell me you *can't* tell me because if you do, it won't be a surprise anymore."

Her mother laughed once again. "You know me too well."

"Impossible." Pamela Delaney Jerome Martinez de la Madrid Touissante Pynchley-Smythe Horowitz was a human kaleidoscope. There were moments when Hayley felt as though she didn't know her at all. "Now, out with it."

"Well, dear, Elliot and I are coming to New York."

"R-really?" Hayley stammered after a second or two.

"Yes, really," came the blithe confirmation. If Pamela found her daughter's reaction less than satisfactory, she gave no indication of it. "In about a month. One of the charities Elliot works with is having a gala fund-raiser in Manhattan the week before Thanksgiving. I didn't say anything when you were out in San Francisco because Elliot didn't think he was going to be able to get away for it. But he's managed to rearrange his schedule. I'm so excited. It'll be marvelous to see you again. And I'm absolutely dying to meet Michael."

Hayley had gone cold. "You want to meet Michael?"

"Of course, I do. After all, he's the closest thing to a son-in-law I've ever had."

"I never said anything about Michael and me getting married!" Even to Hayley's ears, this protest sounded very shrill.

"Oh, I realize that." Pamela's tone was soothing. "But I'm sure it's only a matter or time. Not *too* much time, I hope. After all, you're thirty-two, Hayley. And I'm—well, let's just say I'm gracefully edging toward the age when being called 'granny' isn't going to devastate me."

"Mother—" Dear Lord, Pamela hadn't just mentally married her off to Michael, she had her having children by him as well!

"I know you love him, dear. I can hear it in your voice whenever you talk about him. Frankly, there are times you make him sound too good to be true."

Hayley made a sound that was somewhere between a hysterical giggle and a horrified groan.

"Hayley?" her mother questioned. "Are you all right?"

"I'm fine," Hayley answered quickly, perjuring herself without compunction. "Uh—you've just—uh, well—this whole thing's—uh—"

"Taken you by surprise?"

"Yes. Exactly," Hayley affirmed feelingly, her brain racing. "Now, um, when exactly are you and Elliot planning to be here?"

Her mother reeled off a series of dates.

"Oh." Hayley ran her tongue over her lips. "I'm not certain Michael's going to be in the city then."

"We can fly in a few days earlier, dear."

"Ah—"

"Or stay a few days later."

"I appreciate your willingness to be so flexible, Mother, but I've told you how unpredictable Michael's travel schedule is. You remember what happened last month when he was going to come out to San Francisco with me. We had everything all set, and then his office called just as we were leaving for the airport, and he had to take off for—ah—

for—" Hayley floundered, desperately trying to recall where she'd told her mother Michael had been sent.

"Tierra del Fuego," her mother supplied helpfully.

Tierra del Fuego? Hayley thought. Where in the name of heaven had she come up with that?

"Oh, yes. Tierra del Fuego," she repeated.

"I've always wanted to visit there," Pamela confided. "It sounds so exotic. I hope Michael will tell me all about it. Did he have time to take any pictures?"

"Uh—no. I'm afraid not. He was terribly busy. But back to the point, Mother. Please. You have to understand. I can't promise you'll be able to meet Michael when you come here. In fact, I'm almost positive he told me he was going to have to go out of town the week before Thanksgiving."

"I'm sure with this much advance notice he can work something out. You've said he's very resourceful."

"Well..."

"I really am so excited about—oh, my. There's the doorbell. It must be my friend, Muriel. You've never met her, have you? She's a lovely woman—does all kinds of charity work. But she's a terrible gossip. Always telling people awful things for their own good. I've got to go. And I'm sure you need to get back to work. I'll call you at home tomorrow morning, all right?"

"Great," Hayley responded numbly.

"Take care, dear. And give my best to Michael."

"Oh...I will."

Hayley hung up the phone. Her hands were shaking. Her stomach was churning. She, who prided herself on anticipating every possible contingency, had just been blindsided.

What am I going to do? she asked herself, trying not to hyperventilate. *What am I going to do?*

Well, if worse came to worst—and Hayley had the dismal feeling it was going to—she supposed she could always resort to telling the truth.

"Mother," she'd say calmly, *"I've got a surprise for you. You know Michael Becker, the man you think I'm going to marry? Well...I made him up. He doesn't exist."*

One

───

Nick O'Neill hadn't planned on falling in love with Hayley Jerome any more than he'd planned on getting her drunk and spending the night with her. Things just worked out that way.

They might not have worked out any way at all if his and Hayley's boss, Albert Kozlow, hadn't ordered him to take some time off.

"I'm *what?*" Nick demanded, staring up at the balding, bulky man who was in charge of one of the most successful strike forces in Justice Department history. His well-tuned antenna had started humming the instant Kozlow had lumbered over to his desk. He'd known something was up. Unfortunately none of his guesses about the nature of this something had been anywhere close to being accurate.

"You're out of here for two weeks starting Monday," Kozlow repeated in a gravelly voice, buttoning the front of his tan trenchcoat. "I approved your vacation request Wednesday, right after you finished your testimony in the Callahan case."

"I didn't submit a vacation request, Al," Nick pointed out.

"I submitted one on your behalf."

"Why?"

"Because you haven't had a full day off in more than a year, and it's time you came up for air."

Nick stiffened. "You think I'm losing my edge?"

"Quite the contrary." The older man ran his palm back from his furrowed brow, smoothing his thinning crop of gray hair. "I think your edge is getting a little too sharp."

Nick considered this remark for several moments, reluctantly admitting that there might be a modicum of truth to it. His stepfather, a retired police detective named Deke Walker, had suggested something very similar to him the last time they'd spoken. He wondered fleetingly if Deke had been talking to Al. He was well aware that the two most influential men in his life had been friends for more than three decades.

Nick couldn't deny that he'd had to let it all hang out during his last undercover assignment. Nor could he deny that he was having a bit of trouble getting everything tucked back in now that the bad guys had been busted. There'd been a time when he'd been able to put on and pull off false identities like socks. But at thirty-six, he was finding the chameleon process more and more complicated. He wasn't certain whether this was because his sense of self had gotten stronger over the years or because his identification with the characters he assumed had gotten deeper.

In either case, maybe taking two weeks' worth of R and R was just what he needed, Nick reflected. But, dammit, he didn't like having the idea shoved down his throat! Not even when the person doing the shoving was someone he respected as much as he respected Al Kozlow.

Nick eyed his boss narrowly. "Why didn't you tell me this Wednesday?"

"You mean, why did I present you with a fait accompli at—" Kozlow consulted his wristwatch "—six-forty-eight Friday evening?"

"Yeah."

"Simple. If I'd told you Wednesday, you would have spent yesterday and today trying to con me into changing my mind."

Touché, Nick acknowledged silently, then summoned up his most guileless expression. Not that he expected it to convince the other man. Kozlow had him nailed and numbered this time, and they both knew it.

"I'd never try to con you, Al," he said.

"Of course you would, O'Neill." While the contradiction was cordial, the smile that punctuated it was little more than a baring of teeth. "You try to con everybody. And you get away with it too damned often for your own good."

Nick was mulling over this last comment when he ran into Hayley Jerome about thirty minutes later. He'd just finished squaring away the paperwork he couldn't let slide until he got back from his involuntary vacation, and he was heading for the elevator at a brisk pace. He reached Hayley's office as she was stepping out of it. They collided.

"Sorry," Nick apologized quickly, catching Hayley by the upper arms and steadying her. A faint whiff of her perfume tantalized his nostrils. The scent was clean, crisp, and very classy. He remembered smelling it the first time they'd met, six months before. He'd liked it then. He liked it now. "Are you all right?"

"Fine," Hayley answered automatically, taking a quick step backward. She hadn't been this close to Nick O'Neill since she'd been introduced to him the day after she'd joined the special unit headed by Al Kozlow. The brown-haired, hard-bodied man had had an unnerving effect on her then. He was having an equally unnerving effect on her now. Her pulse had gone from steady to syncopated, and there was a curious fluttering in the pit of her stomach.

"You're here late," Nick commented after a moment, wondering about the uncharacteristic uneasiness he detected in Hayley. Poised, polite, with every hair in place—that was the image she presented to the world. At the moment, however, she was obviously unsettled and slightly disheveled.

"I lost track of the time," Hayley replied uncomfortably. Her glasses felt askew, so she straightened them. She wished she didn't have to tilt her head back to look Nick in the eye. Unfortunately he was a good half-foot taller than her own five-six.

"I see." Nick knew the blond and brainy Miss Jerome was more than a little obsessive about her job. She kept long hours, and she was driven by an uncanny talent for turning the driest of documents into juicy investigative leads. Even so, something told him it hadn't been work that had kept her in the office until nearly seven-thirty on this particular Friday evening.

But if not work—what?

Hayley decided it was time to shift the focus of this exchange. The expression in Nick O'Neill's penetrating hazel eyes was far too assessing for her taste. The last thing in the world she wanted was for this man—for *anyone!*—to discover that she'd spent the past three hours in a daze because her mother was coming to town to meet her imaginary lover.

"What about you?" she asked.

Nick knew a diversionary tactic when he heard one, but he allowed himself to be diverted, at least for the moment. "What about me?"

"You're here late, too," she pointed out.

"Prevacation paperwork." He grinned ruefully. "Our esteemed leader has informed me I'm taking two weeks off starting Monday."

Hayley needed a moment to translate this. "Al's forcing you to go on vacation?"

"He submitted the request himself. Approved it, too. He stopped by my desk on his way out this evening and let me in on the secret."

"You didn't know?" Hayley was genuinely appalled.

"Not a clue. It was a total surprise."

Surprise.

Hayley tried to mask her reaction to the last word. But if the sudden narrowing of Nick's gray-green eyes was anything to judge by, she didn't do a very good job of it.

"You don't like surprises?" he questioned.

Hayley averted her gaze. "No," she answered flatly, knowing it wouldn't do any good to pretend otherwise. Eventually she looked back at Nick. "I suppose you do," she said with an edge.

A shrug. "That depends."

"On—?"

"The nature of the surprise, of course."

There was a pause. Hayley shifted her weight and brushed an errant strand of hair back from her face. It suddenly occurred to her that this was the longest personal conversation she'd ever had with Nick. As a matter of fact, if she excluded generic exchanges of "hellos," "how are yous," and "have a nice days," it was the *only* personal conversation she'd ever had with him.

This dearth of extracurricular contact was not a matter of chance. Hayley had made up her mind within minutes of being introduced to Nicholas James O'Neill that she was going to steer clear of him as much as she could.

Her decision had not been based on antipathy. Just the opposite. She'd taken one look at Nick and experienced a tug of attraction so potent it had temporarily deprived her of the ability to speak. She'd gone weak in the knees when they'd shaken hands. The brief contact—his faintly callused palm pressing against her smooth one—had been like the closing of an electric circuit.

Hayley knew that a lot of women, including her mother, would have reveled in the instant infatuation. She, however, had rejected it. She wanted no part of that kind of unruly emotion or the complications it invariably caused.

Hayley cleared her throat, searching for a graceful exit line. "Well, uh, I guess I'll see you when you get back from your vacation," she said, hoping he'd pick up the hint.

"Yeah," Nick replied automatically, trying to figure out what was going on behind her guarded blue eyes. Hayley Jerome intrigued him. She'd intrigued him from the moment they'd met.

And yet, he'd never made a move on her. Not one. He hadn't even tried to flirt with her. Not really.

Which was a bit strange, considering. He wasn't exactly the shy and retiring type when it came to women. This was not to imply that he was promiscuous. Oh, sure, there'd been a brief period when he'd preferred quantity to quality, but he'd been young and stupid back then. In recent times, he'd been selective to the point of staying celibate for months at a stretch. Even so—

Nick frowned suddenly.

Hell, he thought. Forget about never having made a move on Hayley Jerome! Now that he looked back, he realized he'd never even had a real conversation with her! Professional encounters, yes. Polite exchanges, absolutely. But that was it. He'd suckered himself into thinking he was getting to know the lady because he'd done a little bit of unofficial checking around and a whole lot of observing. The truth was, he was barely acquainted with her.

His fault?

Her fault?

Or simply a combination of circumstances?

Nick couldn't say for certain, although he had some strong suspicions. It didn't really matter. What mattered was that he intended to start rectifying the situation immediately.

He saw Hayley open her mouth to speak. He didn't give her a chance to get a word out.

"Have dinner with me tonight," he said.

"D-dinner?" Hayley stammered. She'd seen Nick's expression change a moment before and braced herself for something, but she'd never anticipated this.

"Yeah."

"Well—"

"Do you have other plans?" he asked quickly. Instinct told him that the key to getting Hayley to accept his invitation was keeping her off balance.

"Uh—no," Hayley found herself maneuvered into admitting. "It's just that—"

"What? You don't want to have dinner with me?"

"I didn't say that."

"Then you *do* want to have dinner with me."

"I didn't say that, either!"

"You don't seem to be saying much, do you?"

"Well—I—if you'd—"

"Let me guess," Nick interrupted smoothly. "You're not hungry."

The truth was, Hayley had skipped lunch and she was starving. But she would have denied it to the bitter end if her stomach hadn't chosen this particular moment to start rumbling emptily.

"Oops. Bad guess," Nick said, suppressing a smile when Hayley glared at him. He paused a beat, then asked, "So? What do you say?"

Hayley took a steadying breath, trying to get her bearings. While she'd had invitations from other members of the strike force, none of them had been pressed as hard as Nick's.

"I say this is . . . very unexpected," she replied.

"And you don't like the unexpected." It wasn't a question.

"Only if I'm prepared for it," she snapped.

Nick lifted a brow at this last retort. His gut told him he'd just been handed a crucial insight into Hayley Jerome's approach to life.

"I see," he said after a moment.

Hayley stiffened. The assessing look was back in Nick's eyes. She hadn't liked it before, she liked it even less now.

"I didn't mean it that way," she told him defensively.

"And what way is that?"

"The way you're thinking."

"I didn't realize you read minds."

Hayley ignored the jibe. "Look, I'm just as capable of spontaneity as you are," she asserted through gritted teeth.

There was a short, sharp pause. Hayley mentally replayed what she'd just said and winced inwardly, recognizing the opening she'd given Nick. She waited tensely for him to take advantage of it.

He didn't.

"Well?" she challenged finally, unable to stand the silence any longer. "Aren't you going to ask me to prove it?"

Nick shook his head. It was impossible to tell what he was thinking. While he had extraordinarily mobile features—like a skilled actor, he seemed able to alter his looks at will—he also possessed the ability to wipe his lean face completely free of expression.

It's a trick, she decided. It has to be a trick.

"Why not?" she questioned warily.

"Because you expect me to."

Hayley gasped at his audacity. Then, to her astonishment, she started to laugh. It was either that, she realized helplessly, or lose her temper completely.

"You—you're impossible!" she declared when she'd recovered enough breath to speak.

Nick's lips relaxed into a roguish grin. A crescent-shaped indentation appeared at the left corner of his mouth. "So I've been told."

"Well, you shouldn't sound so smug about it," Hayley chided, struck by the sudden change in his angularly attractive face.

"Why not?"

She gestured, searching for a reason. "Being impossible is nothing to be proud of."

"Oh, I don't know about that," Nick countered, roguishness giving way to reflection. "It's better than being predictable."

"Which is what you think *I* am." Hayley wanted to recall the words the instant she said them. Good God, why should it matter to her if Nick O'Neill held that opinion of her? she asked herself. After all, she *wanted* to be predictable... didn't she?

Of course, she did!

Heaven knew, it wasn't easy. She was unhappily aware that she had an inclination toward impulsiveness. Whether that trait was inherited or acquired, she couldn't say. Whatever the case, she'd spent years trying to control—if not totally quell—it. She'd finally reached the point where she was successful about ninety-five percent of the time. As for the five percent of the time she failed... well, she just prayed that no one noticed those few occasions when she leaped before she looked.

Nick studied Hayley's face silently for several seconds, his expression enigmatic. "That's what I used to think," he admitted slowly. "But I've changed my mind."

His words triggered an unsettling quiver deep inside Hayley. She clenched her fingers, trying to still their sudden trembling. "And what does that mean?" she asked after a moment.

"Why don't you have dinner with me and find out?" he challenged.

Hayley's lips parted. She felt her cheeks grow warm. She found herself looking up into his compelling eyes and thinking about moths and flames.

"Come on, Hayley," Nick urged. His voice had dropped in pitch and volume. It was dark and deep and dangerously enticing. "Surprise me. Say yes."

In the end, Hayley did. And in doing so, she had the impression she surprised herself a lot more than she surprised him.

Two

They wound up at a corner table in a small, bistro-style French restaurant about four blocks from the building where they worked. Nick sat with his back to the wall. He wasn't comfortable being in a position where anybody could sneak up on him. He also wanted to be able to keep an eye on the exits and entrances.

Nick let Hayley set the conversational tone for most of the meal. She proved to be extremely well-informed about a wide variety of subjects, which he'd expected. She also proved to be possessed of a rather subversive sense of humor, which he had not.

Hayley had acquired a reputation as an Ice Princess since joining the strike force. From what Nick had observed, this reputation was not entirely undeserved. Still, he'd long since come to the conclusion that the Ice Princess persona was only one facet of a very complicated woman.

Nick was determined to discover what the other facets were. *All* of them.

He also wanted to find out the source of the distressed expression that kept flickering across Hayley's face during dinner. He had a hunch it was tied to the reason she'd stayed so late at the office.

Nick finally broached the topic of what was bothering her as they were finishing their entrées. "So, Hayley," he began, topping off her wineglass as he'd done several times before. "What's the problem?"

"What makes you think there's a problem, Nick?" she countered, setting down her knife and fork.

"You keep zoning out," he explained easily, noting that her slender-fingered hands were trembling. Other than that, she seemed to have herself under perfect control. His earlier suspicions about why he'd made so little progress getting to know her during the previous six months intensified. "My ego won't let me believe it's my fault, so there's got to be something serious on your mind."

Hayley picked up her wineglass and took a healthy sip. Nick was struck, not for the first time, by the provocative shape of her mouth. While the rest of her features were coolly classic—the softly arched brows, the delicate nose, the finely molded cheekbones—her mouth was lush. Erotic. Decidedly at odds with the polished, proper aura she projected.

"Talking can help, you know," he observed, shifting in his seat.

Hayley looked at him over the rim of her glass. "Is this how you get criminals to confess things to you?" she asked with a hint of sarcasm, then took another drink. "By telling them it'll help to talk?"

Nick grinned. "Sometimes. And sometimes I threaten to beat the hell out of them if they don't give me the information I want."

Hayley took a third sip of wine. "Really?" The query was slightly slurred.

Nick made a gesture that was open to multiple interpretations, then patiently repeated his original question. "What's the problem?"

Hayley stared across the table at him with big, blue, and no longer bespectacled eyes. She'd removed her glasses shortly after they'd ordered and tucked them away in her purse. Nick had felt a quick of jolt of satisfaction when she'd done so. While he didn't doubt that Hayley needed glasses, he'd had a feeling she also used them to keep people at a distance. There was no disputing that the lenses muted the sparkle in her eyes. Glasses on, she looked very cool. Glasses off...

"Hayley?" he prompted after nearly thirty seconds of silence. Her expression had become rather glazed.

She blinked, focusing on him once again. "My mother and her fiancé are coming to New York the week before Thanksgiving," she announced.

There were two conclusions Nick could draw from this statement. He opted for the most obvious. "You and your mother don't get along?"

Hayley looked shocked at the suggestion. "My mother and I get along wonderfully," she informed him. "She's a wonderful woman."

"Then it's her fiancé you don't want to see."

Hayley shook her head. Her fair, shoulder-length hair shifted with the movement. Nick found himself momentarily distracted by speculation about whether it would feel as soft as it looked. Then Hayley's voice reclaimed his attention.

"Oh, no," she asserted. "Elliot's wonderful, too."

Under normal circumstances, Nick would have been suspicious of Hayley's repetition of the word "wonderful." But these were not normal circumstances. Besides, his instincts told him Hayley was sincere in her use of the adjective. He went back to his initial inquiry once again, hoping that the third time might prove a charm.

"So, what's troubling you?"

Hayley picked up her glass and swallowed the mouthful of wine that remained in it. She stared at the empty glass for several moments, then set it down very deliberately. Nick had the feeling she'd just come to a decision.

"Not what," she corrected. Her diction, which had always been very good, was now precise to the nth degree. *"Who."*

"Excuse me?"

"Michael Becker." She sighed. "My mother and Elliot expect to meet him when they come to New York."

Nick searched his memory. Becker. Becker. He'd helped bust a smuggling ring headed by a guy named *Marty* Becker a few years back. And there'd been a would-be blackmailer named Michael *Barker* on the periphery of the Callahan case. But *Michael Becker?* Nope. That didn't ring any bells.

"Who's Michael Becker?" he asked.

Hayley sighed again and reached for the carafe. "My future fiancé," she declared heavily, then pulled a face. "Or so my mother thinks."

Nick felt as though he'd been kicked in the stomach. *Her future fiancé?*

"I didn't realize you were involved with anyone," he said after a few seconds. His voice was tight. So were the fists he'd clenched his fingers into.

Hayley emptied the carafe into her glass, spilling a few drops of wine onto the red-and-white check tablecloth. "Oh, I'm not," she assured him. "Not really."

"But you just said—"

"Are you sure you want to hear about this, Nick?" she interrupted.

"Yes, dammit!" The words came out a lot more forcefully than he intended. Nick saw several heads turn in the direction of their table. He took a deep breath, fighting to get himself under control. Al had been right, he realized. He *did* need some time off.

When he spoke again, his tone was quiet and careful. "Yes, Hayley," he said. "I'm sure I want to hear about this."

"It's very—" she veiled her eyes with her long lashes, her soft lips twisting "—complicated."

"Terrific. I thrive on complications."

Hayley drank some of her wine, apparently considering where to start. Eventually she said, "I'm thirty-two."

Nick squashed the urge to demand what Hayley's age had to do with anything. He reminded himself that the path to the truth was sometimes extremely circuitous. "Yeah," he said after a brief hesitation. "I know."

Her forehead furrowed. "You do?"

Nick debated with himself, then decided he owed Hayley one or two facts. "I took a look at your personnel file a couple weeks after you joined the strike force," he admitted.

She regarded him owlishly. "Why?"

Her tone wasn't coy. Nick knew coy and all its variations. What he heard in Hayley's single syllable inquiry was curiosity and an odd quality of astonishment. A dozen possible responses ran through his head. More than a couple of them made him remember Al Kozlow's parting crack about his trying to con everybody.

All right, he thought. No conning. The truth.

"Because I'm interested in you, Hayley," he said frankly.

He wasn't certain what kind of reaction he expected from her, but it definitely wasn't the one he got.

"I'm interested in you, too, Nick," Hayley confessed in a solemn voice. A split second later she seemed to register what she'd just said. Her eyes widened and her cheeks went pale. "I mean, I'm interested in you *professionally,*" she clarified. "Not personally. I couldn't be interested in you that way any more than you could be interested in me that way. Oh, no."

Nick remained silent. He wondered what Hayley would say if he told her that, contrary to what she seemed to believe, he'd been interested in her "that way" for nearly six months. He also wondered if she wasn't protesting about the nature of *her* interest in *him* a bit too much.

"Right, Nick?" Hayley asked anxiously.

Every instinct Nick had told him that if he responded honestly, he'd blow his opportunity to find out about Michael Becker. So, he lied.

"Right, Hayley."

She was visibly relieved. "Right," she echoed, then took yet another drink of wine.

"Let's get back to your being thirty-two," Nick suggested after a few seconds. He found himself on the receiving end of a blank stare. "It has something to do with your future fiancé," he prodded.

"Oh. Yes. Michael." Hayley nodded a few too many times. When she finally stopped nodding, she frowned. "Does your mother want you to get married, Nick?"

"I don't see what this has to do with—"

"How old are you?"

Nick cocked his head, assessing Hayley's expression. If she was jerking his chain, it didn't show on her face. All he saw there was an inquiring look.

"I'm thirty-six," he answered after a moment.

"And you've never been married even once, right?"

"Right," he confirmed warily.

"So, does your mother ever—" Hayley gestured expansively, narrowly missing knocking over her wineglass "—you know. Does she ever drop hints about weddings or grandchildren or anything?"

Nick's memory suddenly flashed back to his last telephone conversation with his mother, Anne. "Occasionally," he acknowledged.

Hayley hiccuped. "Well, *my* mother does it *all* the time."

"I see," Nick said slowly. He began trying to put the pieces together. Unfortunately they didn't seem to fit.

And then a breathtakingly bizarre notion popped into his head. It wasn't plausible, of course. Never, in a million years, could it be considered plausible. Yet there was no denying that it linked everything Hayley had said thus far into a coherent . . . one might even say logical . . . whole.

Could it be? he wondered. Could this "future fiancé" with whom she claimed she wasn't really involved possibly be—

No, he decided firmly. Not even *he* would have the nerve to try to pull off the kind of scam that had just occurred to him. And, God knew, nerve was something he had in abundance. The notion that Hayley Jerome might be engaged in the type of deception he was envisioning was utterly ridiculous.

"My mother believes in marriage," Hayley went on. She grimaced. "She's committed it five times."

"*Five?*"

"Her first husband was my father. He died. She divorced the other—uh—four. They're still alive, though." Hayley fell silent, apparently reflecting on the implications of this situation.

"Hayley?" Nick prompted after about ten seconds, squelching a desire to reach across the table and snap his fingers in front of her nose. She'd had—what? Three glasses of wine? No. More than that. Quite a *bit* more than that, in fact. During the early part of the meal, he'd made it a point to keep her glass full. She'd been uptight. He'd wanted to relax her. He'd obviously succeeded ... and then some.

Hayley started. "What?" she asked, sounding slightly alarmed. "What's wrong?"

"Nothing's wrong. You have to finish telling me about your mother's belief in marriage."

"My mother's—oh. That." Hayley nodded. "Yes." She nodded again. "Right. Um...well, my mother's more or less been planning my wedding ever since I was born. It was okay when I didn't get married in my twenties. I mean, she was a little upset about it, but I think she decided I was a late bloomer. Then I turned thirty and she started to get depressed about my still being single. She got even more depressed when I turned thirty-one. And when I hit thirty-two..." Her voice trailed off.

"She thinks there's something wrong with you?"

"With me?" Hayley's eyes widened. "Oh, no. Not with *me*. She thinks there's something wrong with *her*."

"Huh?" Nick prided himself on being able to follow the twists and turns of other people's thought processes. But he was damned if he could track Hayley's...or her mother's.

"She thinks she failed in her maternal duty and doomed me to being unhappily unmarried for my entire life."

While Nick had a great deal of self-control, he didn't have enough to swallow the question that sprang to his tongue. "*Are* you unhappy?" he asked.

"About being single?" The crystalline blue of Hayley's eyes turned chilly. "No. Absolutely not. I don't want to get married. Not *ever*."

Nick said nothing for several moments, hoping she might feel impelled to elaborate on her last statement. She didn't. Which, when he considered it, made sense. After all, she'd already told him that her mother had buried one husband and divorced four others. What else needed to be said?

But what about the "future fiancé?" What about Michael Becker?

"Where does Michael Becker fit into all of this, Hayley?" Nick questioned.

Hayley fiddled with her wineglass. "My mother had a birthday in August, and I wanted to do something extra-special for her. I mean, even though she'd gotten engaged to Elliot in June, she was in a terrible funk because of my, uh, status. So, I thought and thought and thought about what she might want more than anything else in the world. I realized there was only one answer." She glanced at Nick.

"A ... son-in-law?" he guessed.

She nodded.

"So—" he gestured, sketching the scenario "—you went out and found this Michael Becker guy."

The corners of Hayley's mouth drooped and started to tremble. Her eyes took on a suspicious sheen. She sniffed.

"Hayley?" Nick asked, frowning at her change of expression.

"I d-didn't go out and find him," she said morosely, sniffing a second time. "Not the way you're thinking, anyway."

Nick realized with a shock that she was on the verge of tears. He was assailed by a sudden sense of guilt.

You bastard! he berated himself, staring at Hayley's quivering lips and clouded eyes and knowing they were his fault. First you pour her full of wine, then you get her upset by trying to pump her for personal information. You ought to be ashamed of yourself!

Actually he *was* ashamed. Ashamed enough to try to reroute the course of their conversation right then and there.

While he hadn't changed his mind about wanting to get to know Hayley Jerome, he was damned if he was going to do it like this. His code of conduct might be more flexible than a lot of people's, but it wasn't warped!

"Hayley, look, maybe we should—"

"There is no Michael Becker, Nick," she confessed in a rush, giving no indication she'd even registered that he'd spoken. "I made him up because I wanted to make my mother happy. And it was all right until today. I mean, she believed everything I told her about him. Only—only now she's coming to New York, and she expects to meet him!"

It took a lot to render Nick O'Neill speechless, but this anguished outpouring did the trick.

Great God Almighty, he thought, gazing at the woman sitting across from him as though seeing her for the first time. *I was right. She's been scamming her own mother!*

Hayley leaned forward. She planted both elbows on the table and propped her chin on top of her fisted hands. Then she fixed Nick with an unwavering stare.

"I think—hic!—I'm gonna have to kill him," she declared.

"Hayley?" Nick rapped his knuckles against the closed bedroom door. He listened intently.

Nothing.

"Hayley?" He knocked again, more forcefully than the first time.

Still nothing.

Grimacing, Nick raked the fingers of one hand back through his dark brown hair and debated what he should do.

Roughly an hour had passed since Hayley had made her extraordinary admission about Michael Becker. In the wake of that admission, Nick had summoned a waiter and paid their bill, then firmly told his inebriated dining companion that he thought it was time he took her home.

Hayley's endorsement of this plan had been immediate and enthusiastic. But while Nick had been grateful for her amiability, he hadn't viewed it as a sign that the Ice Princess was warming up to him. He'd had the feeling she would have been just as swift to embrace the idea of their going hang gliding off the Empire State Building if he'd suggested that.

Except for Hayley's disconcerting insistence on discussing her plans for "killing" Michael, their taxi ride back to her place had been relatively uneventful. The journey from the entrance of her building to the door of her apartment unit had gone smoothly as well.

There'd been a bit of stickiness when, after spending several frantic minutes rooting through the contents of her purse, Hayley had dramatically announced that they were going to have to call the police because someone had stolen her keys. Having no desire to get into a public argument, Nick had unceremoniously relieved Hayley of her bag and located the allegedly pilfered property in a matter of seconds. He'd then proceeded to ignore her indignant assertions that *she* should be the one to use *her* keys to open *her* door.

Hayley's contentious mood had undergone a lightning-quick change once they'd actually stepped into her apartment. Suddenly she'd become the epitome of sweetness and light. After blithely telling Nick to make himself at home, she'd vanished into her bedroom and shut the door.

Initially Nick had been quite happy to follow Hayley's instructions. That is to say, he'd shed his suit jacket, loosened his tie, and proceeded to snoop around his hostess's ivory and blue living room.

The place was impeccably decorated in a sophisticated blend of ornate antiques and austere modern pieces. It was also immaculately—even intimidatingly—neat. The fringed edges of the room's two Oriental rugs looked as though they'd been combed. The frames of the photographs and prints hung on the wall were all perfectly aligned. The books on the three sets of floor-to-ceiling shelves were organized by subject then alphabetized by author. There wasn't a speck of dust anywhere.

At first glance, it hadn't looked like the living room of a woman who was capable of getting herself entangled in a scheme involving an imaginary lover. But then Nick had glanced a second time…and a third. He'd suddenly seen the whimsical independence in the juxtaposition of old furniture and new. He'd caught the quirky humor in several of the prints, too. He'd also noticed that the books on the shelves weren't limited to "serious" fiction and weighty tomes on law, history, and computer science. There were several volumes of fairy tales and a small, rather battered collection of paperback romances as well.

Interesting, he'd thought, savoring the implications of each of his discoveries. Very…very interesting.

And then he'd glanced at his watch and realized that Hayley had been absent for nearly fifteen minutes. A series of unpleasant possibilities had rushed through his brain. A sense of apprehension had chilled him.

He'd gone to her bedroom door and knocked.

Once.

Twice.

"Hayley?" he questioned, banging his fist against the painted wood for the third time. "It's Nick. Are you all right?"

He put his ear against the door. Dead silence. He couldn't hear a sound from the other side.

Act now, he decided. Apologize later.

Nick opened the door. What he saw made him suck in his breath, then start to curse with quiet intensity.

Hayley lay sprawled on her bed, her fully clothed body as boneless as a rag doll's, her face hidden by a shiny spill of blond hair. Whether she was sleeping, stupefied, or worse, Nick couldn't immediately tell.

Crossing to the bed, he leaned over and gently brushed Hayley's hair back from her face. The strands were silky soft against his fingertips. So was the fine-pored skin of her slightly flushed cheeks.

Hayley didn't stir.

Nick pressed his fingers against the side of her slender neck, searching for her pulse. He experienced a rush of relief when he found it. Thank God. It was strong and steady.

Still, Hayley didn't stir.

Nick withdrew his hand and straightened. He frowned. She seemed all right. She'd probably feel miserable when she woke up, but she seemed to be all right at the moment.

What should he do? he asked himself. Tiptoe out? Maybe leave some kind of note before making his exit?

No, he decided after a few seconds. He couldn't just *go*. He couldn't abandon Hayley and proceed on his merry way. What if she got sick? What if she woke up, tried to go to the bathroom or something, then passed out?

Nick suddenly visualized Hayley lying on the floor with a fractured skull. No, indeed. He very definitely couldn't leave.

Besides. He bore part of the responsibility for Hayley's current condition. While he hadn't forced her to drink that much, he'd certainly done his damnedest to give her the opportunity to overindulge. She'd been distracted and vulnerable, and he'd deliberately taken advantage of that. At the very least, he owed her an apology and an explanation.

Okay. Fine. He'd stay. He'd stay until he was told to get out. And he didn't doubt that "get out" would be one of the first things he'd hear from Hayley once she woke up. He figured she'd say it right after he answered the inevitable question: "What happened?"

Nick studied Hayley's unconscious form. Should he leave her the way she was? Or should he try to make her a little more... comfortable?

There were a number of arguments to be made for—and against—both options. Nick ran through them mentally. His conscience, which tended to operate a bit differently than most other people's, declared itself a neutral party in the debate and endorsed neither course of action.

Finally Nick muttered an expletive and made up his mind. Since Hayley was going to be furious with him anyway...

He took off her shoes, dropping the well-polished calfskin pumps carelessly on the floor. Then he removed her wristwatch and set it on the nightstand at the head of the bed.

So much for the easy stuff.

It took Nick several minutes to ease Hayley out of the tweed jacket she had on over a trim black dress. At one point in the procedure, she started squirming. She murmured something that could have been his name. Nick froze, holding his breath. He exhaled heavily when she finally quieted down. Eventually he resumed his self-assigned task.

Once he finally got the garment off, Nick tossed it across the foot of the bed. Then he stepped back and assessed the situation.

Her dress, he decided after a few seconds. I'll take off her dress and that's it. She can sleep in whatever's underneath.

To Nick's everlasting shock, the "whatever" that was underneath turned out to be a set of red satin lingerie.

And not just any old red, either.

This was red...*hot*...red.

"My God," Nick whispered, acutely conscious of a sudden tightening in his groin.

He'd been aware that Hayley had a taste for pretty underthings. He'd caught a couple of glimpses of lace when she'd crossed or uncrossed her slender legs during briefings. But the lace had always been a ladylike ecru or ivory. Never red.

On another woman, the contrast between fair skin and sizzling scarlet satin might have appeared garish. On Hayley, however, it looked gorgeous—at least as far as Nick was concerned.

"My God," he whispered again, his gaze moving up the long line of her legs, over the womanly curve of her hips, and finally coming to rest on the sweet swell of her beautifully formed breasts. He'd known she had a good figure. Although the clothes she wore in the office certainly didn't emphasize her shape, they didn't disguise the sleek elegance of her body, either. Still, he'd had no idea that she was—

Without warning, Hayley came to. Or, to be more accurate, her eyes popped open.

"Hi, Nick," she said. The salutation was bright. The smile that accompanied it was beaming.

"Hi, Hayley," Nick returned hoarsely. He'd brazened his way through some very awkward moments in his life. He'd also been guilty of more than a few lapses in judgment he hoped nobody ever found out about. But this...this was *really* bad.

He'd been ogling an unconscious woman—a colleague, for pity's sake—in her underwear. What's worse, he probably would have gone on ogling her if she hadn't woken up and caught him at it.

"Do you like my lingerie?" Hayley inquired limpidly.

Nick flushed. He felt mortified. As mortified as the time his mother had discovered him in the bathroom with a girlie magazine. Contrary to what he'd stammeringly tried to tell her afterward, he had not been reading an article on the comparative merits of the world's top sports cars.

There was a lump in his throat the size of a cantaloupe. He swallowed with an audible gulp. "It's very, ah, nice," he managed to reply.

"My mother sent it to me."

"Oh...really?"

"She thought Michael would like it."

"I'm sure he would." Nick's tone was stiff. So was his spine. So was another vital part of his anatomy.

"*If* he existed," Hayley added gravely, then started to giggle. "If—hee-hee-he—hee—hee—ex—hee—hee—isted!" she repeated.

"Hayley—"

"Hee-hee-heemm...hmmm...mmmmmmmmm..." Her eyelids fluttered downward. Her features went slack.

"*Hayley?*"

Hayley didn't answer. She was out like a light once again.

Nick spent the remainder of the night on the couch in the living room. He did not sleep well. The need to check on Hayley's condition woke him up and drove him into her bedroom again and again.

Exhaustion finally claimed him shortly before dawn. He sank into slumber like a stone.

The shrill of a telephone roused him several hours later. He came to with a start, his body tensing, adrenaline flooding his system. He experienced an instant of uncertainty about where he was and how he'd gotten there, then he remembered. He remembered *everything*.

Nick levered himself into a sitting position and glanced around. He spotted what looked like a telephone answering machine sitting on a table about ten feet away. A moment later, he heard Hayley's voice.

"You have reached 555-1503," came the cool but pleasant declaration. "I'm unable to answer the phone right now, but I'd like to know that you called. Please leave your name, number, and a brief message after the beep. Thank you."

BEEP!

"Oh . . . my." The caller was obviously female and obviously flustered. "And here I was hoping that I wouldn't get— Hayley? Dear? This is your mother. In San Francisco. I said I'd call you this morning, remember?"

Afterward, Nick had no memory of consciously deciding to get off the couch and pick up the telephone. He just did it.

"Hello?" he said into the mouthpiece.

There was a shuddery intake of breath on the other end of the line. "Michael?" the woman who claimed to be Hayley's mother asked in a hushed tone. "Is this...Michael Becker?"

Nick went with his instincts. "Yes, ma'am, it is."

Three

Hayley Jerome couldn't imagine how a day that began with her waking up stripped to the most provocative set of underwear she owned and suffering from a hangover of unknown origin could get much worse. Then she walked—well, semi-staggered, actually—into her living room and found out.

"What are *you* doing here?" she croaked, staring in appalled disbelief at the shoeless, sockless, and shirtless man who was sitting on her couch sipping coffee and leafing through a magazine.

Nick O'Neill set down the coffee mug he'd been drinking from, then rose to his feet in a single, seamless movement. His manner was as poised as hers was perturbed. Hayley's befuddled brain began trying to process a myriad of disjointed details about his appearance.

The rumpled state of his thick, dark hair.

The disreputable shadowing of new beard growth on his jaw.

The wrinkled condition of the sole item of clothing he had on.

Comprehension didn't dawn on Hayley. It detonated inside her aching skull like a grenade. He'd spent the night. Merciful heaven, Nick O'Neill had spent the night in her apartment.

But how—?

He'd persuaded her into having dinner with him. Yes. Yes. She remembered that much very clearly. She'd been upset. Unsettled. Not at all her usual self. And Nick O'Neill, master manipulator, undercover operator, had taken advantage of it.

What else had he taken advantage of?

Hayley realized she had absolutely no idea how to answer this question. Her memory of her dinner with Nick was hopelessly blurred. And her memory of what had happened afterward was...was...

It was nonexistent. A blank. She had no recollection of how she'd gotten home to her apartment, much less of how she'd ended up in bed clad in her underwear with makeup still clinging to her skin.

No recollection, but a humiliatingly plausible hypothesis.

Hayley felt herself flush from collarbone to hairline. She clutched at the long white bathrobe she'd put on just a few minutes before.

"Good morning," Nick greeted her. "How are you feeling?"

Hayley ignored the inquiry. She was in no mood for civilities.

"I asked you a question," she returned tautly, clinging to the tattered shreds of her dignity even more desperately than she was clinging to the lapels of her terry cloth robe. She breathed a brief prayer of thanks that she hadn't come stumbling into the living room straight from bed. While she certainly wasn't at her best at this unfortunate moment, she'd at least splashed some water on her face, scrubbed her teeth, and brushed her hair. "What are you doing here?"

Nick shrugged. The casual movement underscored the virile muscularity of his shoulders and upper torso. "I'm making myself at home," he answered laconically. "You told me I should."

Hayley licked her lips. "I . . . did?"

"Mmm-hmm." Nick thrust his hands deep into his pockets and rocked back on his heels. The waistband of his pants dipped for a moment, revealing an expanse of washboard flat belly.

"When was this?"

"Last night. Around eleven-thirty."

"No." Hayley shook her head to emphasize the denial, then winced as her temples started throbbing.

"Yes," Nick countered, flashing a brief grin. The indentation at the left corner of his mouth deepened into a dimple. "It was about—oh, maybe fifteen minutes before I took off your clothes."

A sudden wave of wooziness swept over Hayley. Her knees turned to jelly and she began to sway. Her stomach roiled. For several awful seconds, she was sickeningly certain she was going to throw up.

Nick was by her side in an instant, slipping a supportive arm around her waist. "Easy, Hayley," he soothed. "Just take it easy, angel."

He guided her carefully over to an armchair positioned at an angle to the left of the couch. After helping her lower herself into the seat, he wordlessly urged her back against the well-padded cushions. Hayley shut her eyes and tried to think stabilizing thoughts.

"Better?" Nick inquired eventually, his voice soft. Hayley felt him brush her hair away from her face. His fingertips lingered, feather-light, on the outer rim of her ear.

Hayley opened her eyes. She nodded, struggling to hide the quiver of response Nick's touch evoked within her. His nearness was almost overwhelming. She could feel the warmth of his flesh. Smell the musky, masculine scent of his skin. If she lifted her hand, she would be able to trace the straight line of his nose . . . the arrogant angles of his cheekbones . . . the sensual shape of his mouth . . .

She averted her gaze. Her heart was beating hard and fast. She would have liked to dismiss her reaction as an aberration—as the result of Nick's being half-naked and her being hung over. But she knew she couldn't. She'd experienced this kind of response to him before.

Damn him! Why, of all the men in the world, did Nick O'Neill have to be the one to make her feel this way? Yes, he was attractive. And yes, he was absolutely brilliant at his job. But he was also unorthodox, impetuous, and addicted to risk. She wanted her life to be steady, stable—set in concrete. He, from everything she'd seen and heard, preferred an existence constructed on quicksand.

She organized. Arranged. Planned ahead.

He flew by the seat of his pants so often it was a wonder he didn't have holes in his underwear. Assuming he even bothered with underwear.

They had nothing in common. *Nothing!*

At least . . . nothing she was willing to acknowledge.

Hayley drew a shaky breath, hating the sense of vulnerability she was experiencing at this moment. She shifted her body, trying to put a little physical distance between her and Nick. It wasn't much, but she felt she had to do something.

Nick seemed to sense her intention. The instant she started to ease away from him, he withdrew his hand and took a step back. After a moment, he crossed to the couch and seated himself.

Neither of them said anything for at least fifteen seconds. Hayley knew Nick was watching her. She could feel the weight of his scrutiny.

"You don't remember what happened last night, do you?" he asked finally.

Although his tone was gentle, not judgmental, Hayley couldn't prevent herself from stiffening with shame. She shook her head briefly, knotting her fingers together in an effort to keep them from trembling. Then, gathering her nerve, she turned her head and met Nick's gaze once again.

"Just tell me the worst," she said flatly.

After a moment, he did.

* * *

"You what?" Hayley asked in a shaky voice. Somehow she'd managed to make it through Nick's succinct recitation of what had—and hadn't—happened the night before without being completely overcome by abject humiliation or outraged anger. But this...Lord. This was too much.

"I told your mother I was Michael Becker," Nick repeated.

"How *dare* you!"

"Well, what did you want me to do? She asked me if I was Michael Becker and I said yes. If I'd said no, you'd've been stuck explaining why you were two-timing your nonexistent future fiancé."

Hayley glared at him. "Why did you pick up the phone in the first place?" she demanded. "Why didn't you just let the answering machine take care of it?"

Nick had been very glib up until this point. He'd had fast and facile answers for every question she'd flung at him. But now, suddenly, he seemed at a loss for words.

"I don't know," he said finally. Hayley saw an odd expression flicker through the depths of his hazel eyes. It was gone too quickly for her to put a name to it. Too quickly, in fact, for her to be absolutely certain it had been real.

"You don't know?" she echoed scornfully after several seconds.

"It was an impulse."

She grimaced.

"Haven't you ever acted on impulse?"

Hayley lifted her chin. "Not if I could help it."

There was a brief silence.

"You know," Nick said eventually, "it's not such a bad idea."

There was a testing-the-waters quality to his tone that made Hayley very wary. "What? Acting on impulse?"

"Oh, there's something to be said for that, too," Nick acknowledged, his lips curving into a smile that had an unsettling effect on her breathing. Then he went on, "But I was talking about my pretending to be Michael Becker."

Hayley searched Nick's angular face feature by feature. He means it, she thought. He genuinely means it!

"No," she said flatly, shaking her head.

"Why not?"

"Because."

"Don't you think we could pull it off?"

"*We?*" Her voice soared and split on the word.

"Yes. We. You and—"

"I know what 'we' means, Nick!" she hissed. "I also know that I am not going to let you run some kind of con game on my mother!"

"For heaven's sake, what do you think *you've* been doing?"

"I—that's—why, you—"

"Look, I'm not being critical. To tell the truth, I'm impressed."

Hayley stopped sputtering and stared at Nick, momentarily dumbstruck.

"Impressed?" she finally managed to get out.

He nodded. "That's why I want to help you."

"By pretending to be Michael Becker."

"Exactly."

"You're crazy." She fought to keep her tone reasonable. Rational. As close to normal as possible.

"Hayley—"

"No. I mean it, Nick. You're absolutely crazy."

Nick cocked a brow, his expression ironic. "This from a woman who's in a panic because her mother's coming to town to meet a prospective son-in-law who doesn't exist?"

"I am not in a panic!" Hayley denied furiously, her moderation of just a moment before going right out the window. "I have everything under control. I created Michael Becker. I'll get rid of him."

"How? By shipping him off to Tierra del Fuego again?"

Hayley felt herself go pale. While Nick had made it clear that her tongue had been loose the night before, he hadn't indicated it had been wagging from both ends! Ye gods. Just how much had she told him?

"What—what do you know about Michael going to Tierra del Fuego?"

"Damned little." Nick's expression was rueful. "The first I heard of it was when your mother asked me how I enjoyed my trip."

Hayley closed her eyes. "Oh...no."

"Oh, yes. I did some fast verbal tap dancing, then changed the subject to how much I was looking forward to meeting her."

Hayley opened her eyes. Her temples were beginning to pound again. She felt as though a horde of tiny, drumbeating monsters had taken up residence inside her head.

"I was very convincing," Nick assured her.

"I'm sure you were."

"There's one reason I think I can help you with this situation."

"Because you're better at lying to my mother than I am?"

"Because I learned a long time ago that the key to a successful scam is simplicity. Anything having to do with Tierra del Fuego is too complicated. And as for this idea you've got about killing Michael—"

Suddenly one section of the wine-induced fog that had been balking Hayley's efforts to recall the events of the night before lifted.

She was sitting next to Nick in the back of a taxi. Well, no. Not sitting. She was *leaning* against him, with her head lolling on his shoulder. She was acutely conscious of the toned resilience of his body and the woodsy scent of his cologne. He had his arm around her, and he was trying to persuade her to be quiet. But she wasn't paying the slightest bit of heed. Oh, no. She was too intent on telling him—and anyone else within earshot—why she'd decided that Michael Becker had to be obliterated from the face of the earth.

"Oh, God!" Mortified beyond endurance by this revelation about her behavior, Hayley slumped forward and buried her face in her upturned palms.

She never had any idea how long she remained in this posture, wallowing in the conviction that she'd made a complete fool of herself. Eventually, however, she became aware of the soothing stroke of Nick's hand against her hair. She shivered a little when she felt his fingertips move across her nape. Slowly she lifted her head and looked into his eyes.

They weren't simply a mix of gray and green, she realized with an odd sense of wonderment. They contained rich flecks of chocolate brown and glinting filaments of antique gold as well. And at this particular moment, they also held a remarkable amount of warmth.

"I'm sorry, Hayley," Nick told her quietly.

"For what?" she countered, astonished.

His mobile mouth twisted. "I'm sure you can come up with something. Meantime, why don't I go find you a couple of aspirins. You look like you could use them."

"So?" Nick said on a questioning inflection.

"So," Hayley responded slowly, "I'm embarrassed by what happened."

Roughly forty-five minutes had passed since her emotional outburst. During that time she'd showered and gotten dressed. She'd also gulped down a hangover remedy Nick had whipped up in the kitchen while she'd been pulling herself together.

"What's in this?" she'd asked, wondering if the mud-colored contents of the glass she'd just been handed could possibly taste as vile as it looked.

"Trust me," the concoction's creator had riposted, winking.

Trust him?

Trust the man who'd poured her full of wine, ferreted out her most intimate secrets, and taken off nearly all her clothes?

Trust Nick O'Neill?

The bizarre thing was, she was beginning to.

"Embarrassed, hmm?" Nick echoed thoughtfully, stretching his long, lean legs out in front of him. They were sitting in her living room once again. He on the sofa, she back in the armchair.

"Very."

He smiled a little. "Well, that's what you get for leading such an exemplary life. Every minor slip seems like a major fall from grace."

Hayley considered this assessment silently, wondering why his choice of the word "exemplary" nettled her so much.

"Are you worried that I'm going to say something to somebody about what happened last night?" Nick questioned after a few seconds.

The inquiry—and the intensity with which it was asked—caught Hayley by surprise. "No," she responded after a moment, brushing at an errant lock of hair. "No. Of course not."

"But you were." He shifted his position and leaned forward, his gaze fixed on her face. His forehead was creased with concern, and tension was evident in the lines of his body.

Hayley hesitated, recalling the horrified shock she'd felt when she'd walked into the living room and discovered him sitting on her couch. Lord, that seemed so long ago!

"Well...yes," she conceded. She couldn't pretend that the appalling possibility of her intemperate behavior becoming grist for the office gossip mill hadn't occurred to her.

"What changed your mind?"

Hayley cocked her head to one side, conscious of the rippling of her hair against the back of her neck. "I'm not sure," she admitted honestly. "I just know you won't tell anyone."

Nick relaxed visibly, the set of his neck and shoulders easing, the skin of his brow smoothing out. "Good," was all he said.

A few moments of silence slipped by. Hayley picked a piece of lint off the fawn-colored corduroy slacks she'd put on. Her thoughts darted in a dozen directions, ultimately colliding with the memory of a peculiar comment Nick had made.

"What did you mean when you said you were impressed?" she asked without preamble.

Nick looked puzzled.

"Before. When we were talking about my—" Hayley instinctively shied from the obvious phrase, then forced herself to use it "—about my running a con game on my mother. You said you were impressed."

"Oh." A brief smile. "That."

"Yes. That. What did you mean?"

"Exactly what I said." Nick rubbed one hand against his hair-whorled chest. Although he'd finally put his shirt back on, he hadn't bothered to button it up. "Plenty of people talk about loving their parents and wanting to make them happy. But you—you've done a lot more than talk."

"Oh, right." Hayley pulled a face. "I've made a complete mess of things."

"I wouldn't go that far."

"Maybe not. But I would ."

"So why don't you reconsider letting me help you?"

Hayley didn't respond immediately. The truth was, she *had* reconsidered it. She'd had several weak moments in the shower when she'd seriously thought about accepting Nick's offer of assistance. But her good sense had won out in the end.

At least, she thought it was her good sense. Maybe her instinct for survival was closer to the mark.

"It wouldn't work, Nick," she said. "Thank you, but no."

"Your mother bought me as Michael when I talked to her on the telephone."

"I know she did. And I'm sure she'd buy you as Michael if you met her face-to-face, too."

"Then what's the problem? Are you afraid she'd take a look at me and decide I'm a prospective mother-in-law's worst nightmare?"

Hayley was startled into laughter. If she was afraid of anything, it was exactly the opposite. "Don't I wish!" she gasped. "I mean, that would certainly solve my problem with..."

Hayley's voice trailed off as she saw Nick's eyes blaze up and his lips curve slowly into a smile. He looked like a carnivore contemplating a feast of raw filet mignon.

"...Michael Becker," she concluded faintly. Her heart was hammering and her breath was coming in quick little pants. She knew what Nick was thinking. Good God, she knew exactly what he was thinking!

And he knew she knew. She was absolutely certain of it. She could see it in his face.

"Well?" Nick queried, lifting a brow.

"You said my mother liked you when you talked to her on the telephone," she said quickly, putting forward the first objection that came to mind.

"I said she believed I was Michael Becker," he corrected immediately. "Besides, I was on my best behavior."

"But I've told her all about Michael, Nick! I've made him sound almost perfect."

Nick chuckled. The sound seemed to feather along Hayley's nerve endings. It triggered a quicksilver tingling up and down her spine.

"Hayley, come on. Love is blind. Haven't you ever had a friend who fell for a man she swore was a dream, only when you finally got to meet him you discovered he was a total disaster?"

Hayley hesitated, then gave a reluctant nod.

"Fine. Hold that thought. Now, you told me last night that your mother desperately wants you to get married. Yes?"

"Y-yes." While Hayley didn't actually remember telling him any such thing, the statement was basically correct.

"But she wants you to get married to the *right* man, doesn't she?"

"Well, yes, but—"

"I mean, she's not so desperate that she'd shove you down the aisle with just anybody."

"No. Never. But—"

"In fact, she'd probably stand up and object in the middle of your wedding ceremony if she thought you were making a mistake, right?"

"Yes. Right." Hayley couldn't help noticing that Nick had drawn an uncannily accurate bead on her mother's character on the strength of a single phone conversation.

While she'd known that his undercover work required him to read people's true natures quickly and completely, she'd never realized exactly how sharply honed his powers of perception were.

"So, what do you suppose she'd do if she met Michael Becker and decided he was Mr. Wrong?"

The answer was obvious. "She'd tell me to get rid of him."

"Exactly." He nodded to underscore the point. "And who knows? She might even start to think that if Michael Becker is your idea of a perfect mate, you'd be better off staying single."

Hayley didn't speak for several moments. It was such an alluring idea. Sophisticated, yet simple. And if it worked...

No. She couldn't. The risks were far too great.

"I can't let you get involved in this, Nick," she said finally.

"I'm already involved, Hayley."

This assertion brought her up short. Then she shook her head. "In that case, I can't let you get any *more* involved."

"Not even if I want to be?"

Hayley studied Nick silently. While he met her searching gaze steadily, his expression was impossible to decipher. She was suddenly reminded of the way he'd looked when she'd asked him why he'd picked up the phone and spoken to her mother.

"Why?" Her question was a tentative step into uncharted territory.

"It might be fun."

Hayley didn't know what to say. It was strange. A day ago—barely an hour ago—she would have accepted this explanation without giving it a second thought. It would have fit very neatly with her perception of who Nick O'Neill was and how he operated. But now...

"I'd make a great Mr. Wrong, Hayley," Nick added provocatively.

She had to smile. "I'll bet."

"And, of course, I'm always ready to do a favor for a friend."

Her smile faded. "We're hardly friends, Nick."

"That can change."

"I don't think—"

"But, in the meantime, we can call my helping you out a professional courtesy to a colleague. Okay?"

Hayley hesitated.

Nick leaned forward, his expression intent, his energy focused. "Look. I'm facing a vacation I don't want to take. I've got fourteen empty days to fill. I know what I'm like when I don't have anything constructive to do. Believe me, it's not a pretty sight. You'd be keeping me out of trouble if you said yes."

"Well . . ." She was wavering and she knew it.

"Your mother and her fiancé aren't coming into town until—when? The week before Thanksgiving?" he went on persuasively. "That gives us some leeway. Let's improvise and see what we come up with. If you've still got misgivings when it comes time for me to go back to work, we'll drop the whole thing. What do you say?"

A laugh tickled the back of Hayley's throat. She struggled to suppress it. She suddenly felt lightheaded, even a little giddy. "Why do I have this nagging suspicion that I'm being conned into something?" she inquired, knowing there was capitulation—even complicity—in her voice.

Nick smiled, shards of green and gold sparking in his eyes. "Because you have terrific instincts."

Four

Two days later Hayley sat at her desk pretending to work. What she was really doing was waiting for a telephone call from a man who didn't exist.

She was also contemplating the very real possibility that she'd lost her mind. Somehow, insanity struck her as the only sane explanation for her decision to go along with what Nick O'Neill had dubbed "Operation: Mr. Wrong."

Hayley shifted restlessly. She picked up a sheaf of computer printouts, shuffled through the flimsy pages carelessly, then chucked them into her OUT box. She felt itchy. Twitchy. As though her skin didn't quite fit. Her mood oscillated from euphoric to apprehensive and back again. One moment she was soaring with confidence, the next she was earthbound by doubt.

She pulled off her glasses and massaged the bridge of her nose. Why hasn't he called? she asked herself. He said he'd call me this morning!

Or, rather, Nick had said "Michael Becker" would call her this morning to arrange a date.

"You want me to go out with you?" she'd asked uneasily after he'd outlined his idea shortly before they'd parted ways on Saturday.

"No, I want you to go out with Michael Becker."

"You pretending to be Michael Becker, you mean."

"Forget the pretending, Hayley. It's got to be real."

"How many times are we going to have to do this?"

"It depends on how long it takes us to get the right Mr. Wrong."

She'd mulled this over for a few seconds before asking, *"Exactly what do you expect me to do?"*

"I don't 'expect' anything."

His inflection had made her flash back on the conversation they'd had in the corridor outside her office.

"You want me to surprise you?" she'd suggested eventually.

"You said you could be just as spontaneous as I can."

Hayley had seen a gleam in Nick's eyes at this point and realized she was being baited. She'd known she should back off right then, but something inside her had demanded that she stand her ground.

"No problem," she'd returned in a dulcet tone.

Hayley grimaced.

No problem.

Somehow, she doubted it.

She put her glasses back on, shoving them into position with an impatient thrust of her finger. Then she glanced balefully at the telephone sitting on the corner of her paper-strewn desk and thought about the clichéd warning that watched kettles never boil.

Maybe Nick's tardiness in phoning was supposed to be part of his "Mr. Wrong" persona, she reflected darkly. Maybe he envisioned Michael Becker as the kind of man who would promise a woman he'd call but never did.

"Ring," she muttered, glaring at the telephone. "Will you please just—"

"Jerome?"

Hayley nearly jumped out of her chair. "Al!" she gasped, staring at the man who'd materialized in her doorway. She prayed her expression didn't look as guilty as it felt.

"Problem?" her boss inquired in his gravel-gruff voice.

"Oh, no. No. Of course not. Everything's fine. Why do you ask?"

"I heard you talking to yourself."

Hayley manufactured a laugh that tinkled like cheap glassware. "Oh, I do that all the time. I just usually keep the door shut."

"Really." Kozlow advanced into her office with a ponderous tread, coming to a halt directly in front of her desk. He poked at the pile of computer printouts she'd dumped into her OUT basket and grunted as though making some kind of mental note.

Hayley swallowed and forced herself not to squirm. Glancing around, she suddenly realized how messy her normally meticulous workspace was. It reminded her fleetingly of the way her kitchen had looked after Nick had finished fixing the hangover remedy he'd given her. While the concoction had turned out to possess remarkable curative powers, she couldn't help wondering whether it had been absolutely necessary to pillage her cabinets and plunder her refrigerator in order to produce it.

"Ah—is there something I can do for you, Al?" she questioned after a moment or two, fighting down an urge to pop up and start tidying.

Kozlow made a neutral sound. "You still dead-ended on that money laundering trace?" he countered.

Hayley relaxed a little at the switch to a professional topic. "At the moment," she conceded.

"Need help?"

She gestured. "Can you persuade the Cayman Islands to rewrite their banking disclosure laws?"

Kozlow snorted, wordlessly acknowledging his comprehension of the kind of stonewall she was up against. "It's on my list of things to do," he promised with a sardonic smile. "Right after I—"

At that point, the telephone rang. Hayley flashed an apologetic smile at her boss and picked up the receiver.

"Extension 2976," she said.

"Is this, um, Hayley Jerome?"

The voice was Nick's . . . yet not Nick's. Nick's voice was resonant and abundantly expressive. This voice was flat and lacking in vitality. It also had an annoying, adenoidal undertone.

"Yes," Hayley responded carefully.

"This is, um, Michael Becker."

"Oh." Hayley didn't know what else to say. She'd done a fair bit of speculating about the kind of "Mr. Wrong" Nick would pretend to be for their first encounter. The tentative voice coming through the line didn't jibe with any of the possibilities she'd envisioned.

"I'm calling, um, about our, um, date."

Hayley darted a quick look at Al Kozlow. He was making no effort to disguise his interest in her side of this conversation.

"I'm a little busy right now . . . Michael," she responded, pointedly stressing the name. She hoped the man on the other end would still pick up the hint.

The man on the other end did. After a moment, she heard a chuckle. There was no doubt about whose chuckle it was.

"I take it you're not alone," Nick said.

"Definitely not."

"With that tone, it's got to be Al."

"Umm-hmm."

"Okay, then. I'll make this quick. Dinner tonight at seven." He provided the name and address of a restaurant not too far from Hayley's apartment. "Come as you are."

Her heart skipped a beat. "What does that mean?"

"Whatever you want it to. See you at seven."

The next thing Hayley heard was the hum of a dial tone.

"Anyone I know, Jerome?" her boss rumbled.

Frowning, Hayley slowly placed the telephone receiver back in its cradle. "Good question."

* * *

How does he do it? Hayley wondered with appalled fascination as she watched "Michael Becker" attempt to flag down their waiter for the fourth time. The server sailed by without so much as a sideward glance.

Nick O'Neill was one of the most magnetic men Hayley had ever met. Yet he'd somehow transformed himself into a fellow who couldn't attract lint, much less somebody's attention.

The Michael Becker she'd dined with this evening wasn't merely retiring. He wasn't simply reticent. No, he had a personality that receded more obviously than the chins of certain members of Europe's inbred aristocracy!

"Um—um—" the salutation was barely audible, the hand gesture that accompanied it unassertive. The waiter breezed by yet again.

"Oh, *fudge,*" Michael Becker sighed, wilting in his seat like an unwatered plant.

Hayley started to snicker. She couldn't help herself. Although the prissy expression was exquisitely in character, it was just too absurd to hear it issuing from a man she knew had a multilingual command of profanity.

She bit her lower lip, striving for control, reminding herself of the part she was supposed to be playing this evening. She probably would have maintained her composure if her dinner partner hadn't chosen that moment to break character for the first time since they'd sat down.

Michael Becker vanished in the quirk of an eyebrow.

"What's the matter, Hayley?" Nick inquired sardonically. "Haven't you ever heard anyone use the f-word before?"

That did it. Hayley's self-discipline dissolved. She leaned back in her chair and laughed until she ran out of breath.

"I—I'm s-s-sorry," she sputtered after nearly a minute. It had been a long, long time since she'd permitted herself the luxury of letting go as she just had. She inhaled on a series of gasps. "R-really."

"You were handling things like a pro," Nick told her. "But you blew the gaff by breaking up."

Hayley picked up her napkin and dabbed at the outer corners of her eyes. "I blew the what?"

"The gaff. The con." He altered his posture and suddenly looked much taller and tougher. The gray suit jacket he had on went from saggy to sleek. "It's slang."

"I don't think I've ever heard the word before." She crumpled the napkin and dropped it onto the table, then adjusted her glasses and patted at her hair.

Nick shrugged a pair of shoulders that seemed to have broadened by several inches during the past few seconds. "Yeah, well, we grew up in very different circles."

Hayley frowned, not certain of how to interpret this comment. In a peculiar way, it was one of the most intimate things Nick had ever said to her. It made her curious... yet cautious.

She'd gotten an earful about Nick O'Neill since she'd joined the strike force. Not that she'd actively sought information about him. She hadn't. She'd just... listened. And while most of the talk she'd listened to centered on Nick's undercover exploits, she'd picked up a few tidbits about his rather unusual family background, too.

The urge to find out whether these tidbits were true was suddenly very strong. But so was the recognition that she'd be trespassing on potentially treacherous territory if she voiced the question now trembling on the tip of her tongue.

Nick seemed to divine her dilemma. "It's all right to ask, Hayley," he said. "God knows I owe you a few shots after Friday night."

She blushed at the reference to her wine-sodden lack of discretion but decided to take him at his word. "I was only wondering... what you just said about our growing up in different circles—" she began haltingly.

"You don't have to waltz around it," he interrupted. "My parents were con artists. In my softheaded moments I like to think there was as much art as con in what they did, but the truth is my father never earned an honest dollar in his life." His mouth twisted. "He only stopped scamming people because his heart gave out and he died."

"How old were you?"

"Thirteen."

"What happened to your mother?"

"Oh, she stopped scamming because she fell in love with a New York City cop named Deke Walker. She married him twenty-one years ago last March, and she's so law-abiding these days she doesn't even jaywalk."

"And you?" Hayley asked after a moment. She was conscious of a curious tightness in her chest. The sensation became more acute when Nick's gaze met hers.

He smiled suddenly, and she found herself remembering the first time they'd been introduced.

The response she'd felt.

Eyes locking. Fingers clinging. The hop-skip-jump of her heart. The honeyed weakness in the lower half of her body.

The decision she'd made.

Shut down. Steer clear. Stay away.

Lord. She'd been right to question her sanity this morning! *What was she doing with this man?*

"I'm still scamming people," Nick told her softly. "I also tend to run whenever I see signs that say 'Don't Walk.'"

And with that, he raised his right hand and signaled the same server who'd ignored all previous attempts to summon him. Nick didn't say a word. He simply crooked his index finger.

The waiter tripped in his rush to get over to their table.

The Ice Princess—or a reasonable facsimile thereof—was back and Nick was feeling very frustrated about it.

Damn, he thought, slanting a covert glance at Hayley's carefully composed features. While the smooth swing of her pale hair and the turned up collar of her navy trenchcoat obscured part of her cameolike profile, he could see enough of her face to gauge her mood.

They'd left the restaurant a few minutes before and were now walking east toward Hayley's apartment building. Neither of them had spoken a word since they'd emerged into the cool night air.

What had gone wrong? he asked himself. Hayley had been loose and laughing, obviously enjoying the game they were playing. And then, whammo! She'd suddenly pulled back and barricaded herself behind a series of defenses he was still trying to figure out.

Had it been his remarks about his parents that had triggered her withdrawal? he wondered. It didn't seem possible that she could have been unaware of his checkered background. The story of his misspent youth was no secret within the strike force and Hayley had said two or three things during dinner that had revealed she kept her ears open at work. Still, maybe...

No, he decided. The reason—or reasons—for Hayley's retreat ran much deeper than a reaction to his less-than-perfect pedigree. She'd been on guard against him from the very beginning. Having spent a significant chunk of time reviewing the six months of their acquaintanceship, he was now absolutely certain of that. It didn't matter that she'd held herself aloof from everyone else around the office, too. As far as he could tell, there had been nothing personal in that aspect of her strictly business attitude. But when it came to the way she'd kept *him* at arm's length...

His gut told him that was personal. Very, very personal.

Nick would have understood the situation if he'd believed that Hayley had taken an instant dislike to him. Whether he would have accepted it was an entirely different matter. Somehow, he didn't think so. He was too intrigued by—too attracted to—the lady not to have made an effort to alter her opinion of him.

But the thing was, he didn't believe she disliked him. Of course he didn't necessarily believe she liked him, either. What he *did* believe was that Hayley Jerome was anything but indifferent to him.

Nick had glimpsed a brief flare of emotion in Hayley's face the first time they'd met. While he hadn't known how to interpret the expression, it had made a vivid impression on him. He'd seen the same look flash across her features this evening just before she'd gone all prim, proper, and pokered up.

She'd been afraid. Both times, she'd been afraid.

But of what?

He didn't know. But he was damned certain he was going to find out.

Nick shifted his gaze to the right once again. Hayley was staring straight ahead. She couldn't have been any more self-contained if she'd been stuck inside a hermetically sealed plastic bottle.

"So, what did you think of Michael Becker?" he asked, keeping his tone casual.

Hayley's control was extremely good but not perfect. Nick saw her jaw fret. "He...wasn't what I expected," she answered after a moment.

"Glad to hear it." Nick allowed a tinge of smug satisfaction to color his voice. The smugness was manufactured. The satisfaction wasn't. He'd set out to throw Hayley a curve this evening, and obviously had.

Her head snapped left. "What's that supposed to mean?"

"You tell me, I'll tell you."

She came to a halt, chin cocked, posture suddenly confrontational. The silvery-blue light from a nearby street lamp reflected briefly in the lenses of her glasses.

"Excuse me?" she queried pointedly.

Nick stopped, too. "Tell me what kind of Mr. Wrong you expected me to pretend to be tonight," he invited. "A wiseguy, maybe? Somebody with a don't-mess-with-me swagger and a stone-cold mindset?" A slight tightening of her soft lips told him that his guess had been dead on target. "Then again, maybe you didn't expect I was going to have to pretend. Maybe you thought—"

Nick never had a chance to finish the sentence. Suddenly Hayley was in his arms. Not of her own volition, though. Somebody shoved her, sending her slamming into him. He staggered backward, nearly losing his balance.

Afterward, Nick berated himself for having dropped his guard. Normally he would have spotted the greasy-haired punk who'd pushed Hayley coming a block away. But not this time. No, this time he'd been too engrossed in a pair of blue eyes to pay attention to his surroundings.

He understood, with nightmarish clarity, that the consequences of his failure to stay alert could have been infinitely worse than they turned out to be. But this understanding did nothing to alleviate his feelings of guilt. He'd put Hayley at risk and that was all there was to it.

"Are you all right?" he demanded urgently, gripping Hayley's arms. She was pale and obviously shaken. He heard her inhale on a shuddery breath. "Are you?"

"Y-yes," she responded, struggling a little against his hands. "I d-don't need—"

At that moment, a portly, middle-aged man came staggering up. He was red in the face and huffing and puffing.

"Thief," he gasped. "Took . . . took my wife's purse."

Nick swore. "Stay here," he told Hayley. "Look out for her," he told the older man.

Then he took off.

Hayley wanted to hit him.

Didn't Nick realize what a foolhardy thing he'd done? she wondered angrily. Never mind that he'd chased down and captured the drugged-out teenager who'd snatched a purse to pay for his habit. Never mind that the police had arrived in a very timely fashion and hauled the offender away. Never mind that the two of them were now standing safely outside the entrance to her apartment building. So many things could have gone so terribly wrong. He might have been hurt . . . or worse.

Didn't he care?

"He had a knife, Nick!" she said through gritted teeth.

Nick shrugged. "Not for long."

Hayley realized she was shaking. She clenched her hands, trying not to contemplate the horror of what might have been. The memory of what had actually happened was awful enough.

Nick had caught up with his quarry on a side street about four blocks from the scene of the crime. Hayley knew this because she hadn't stayed put as she'd been ordered to. Once she'd realized what Nick intended to do, she ran after him as fast as her high-heeled pumps had permitted.

She'd come stumbling around a corner just in time to see Nick tackle the youth he'd been chasing. The two of them had gone crashing into a group of garbage cans clustered on the edge of the sidewalk.

The teenager had scrambled to his feet first, a knife blossoming from his right fist. Nick had come off the pavement a half second later, lightly balanced on the balls of his feet. He'd been in a semicrouch, arms spread, hands extended palms up, fingers beckoning.

Even from a half block away, Hayley had been able to tell that Nick was urging the purse snatcher to come and get him. She'd watched, terrified, as his ruthlessly calculated taunting had provoked a violent response.

The youth had lunged, his knife blade flashing with coldly lethal intent.

Nick had sidestepped, pivoted, then attacked with feral fluidity.

It had been over very, very quickly.

"What if you'd missed when you kicked him?" she demanded.

"I didn't."

"What if he'd had a gun?"

"He didn't."

"My God, Nick! Don't you realize you could have been *killed?*" Her voice cracked on the last word.

"The possibility crossed my mind once or twice."

Hayley made an inarticulate sound of distress and just barely stopped herself from stamping her foot on the sidewalk. Damn his macho smugness! Damn the chance he'd taken!

"Watch it, Hayley," Nick warned mockingly. "I might get the idea you care about what happens to me."

Hayley went rigid at his provocative words. "Of course I care," she said tightly. "You're my colleague."

"I see."

Hayley didn't like the insinuating quality that had entered his tone. "Do you think it would be easy explaining to Al Kozlow how you got knifed while you were out on a date with me?"

Nick's brows went up. "Worried about awkward questions, hmm?"

"I—"

"Or maybe it's the idea of having to make up the awkward answers that bothers you."

"You—"

"Then there'd be all that paperwork to fill out," he went on reflectively, slowly lifting his hands and cupping her face. "Of course, you're very good with paperwork, aren't you? It's so...predictable."

"Nick—" Hayley heard both plea and protest in the way she spoke his name. She knew it was time to step back, to stop him, to go inside. But she couldn't.

No. It was worse than that. She could, but she didn't want to.

Hayley drew an unsteady breath as Nick carefully eased her glasses off the bridge of her nose and slid them up on top of her head. His fingers lingered briefly in her hair, then trailed lightly down to trace the curves of her cheeks. His eddying touch brought a feverish warmth to her skin.

"What are you so afraid of, Hayley?" he whispered.

She blinked. Although his question was soft, the look in his changeable gray-green eyes was anything but.

"N-nothing," she denied, hating the tremulousness in her voice. "I'm not afraid of anything."

"Yes, you are," he contradicted, caressing the corners of her mouth with his thumbs. "The only question is whether you're afraid of me." He lowered his head a bit. "Or yourself." He lowered it a bit more. "Or both of us together."

Nick's mouth hovered a half inch above Hayley's for a brief, breathless instant. Then, very deliberately, he kissed her.

At age thirty-two, Hayley Jerome was neither innocent nor ignorant. Still, she was unprepared for the surge of desire she felt when Nick's warm and questioning lips began to move against hers.

Slowly, subtly, he coaxed her to open to him. She succumbed to his erotic expertise, shuddering when he pressed his advantage with a gliding stroke of his tongue.

The taste of him was intoxicating.

The smell of him hazed her brain.

Hayley didn't know how long the kiss lasted. It wasn't the sort of experience that could be measured in ordinary increments of time. She only knew that her head was spinning and her blood singing when Nick finally lifted his mouth from hers. Her eyelids fluttered open and she stared up at him.

"How do you feel about mud wrestling?" he asked huskily.

"Wh-what?" She discovered she'd brought her hands up and slid them beneath his jacket. Her fingers splayed against the fine white fabric of his shirt then flexed into the tautly muscled flesh beneath. She could feel the beating of his heart. It was only a shade less rapid than the pounding of her own.

He repeated his question, his breathing ragged.

"Why?"

Nick charted the line of her jaw with his fingertips. "Because the Michael Becker you're meeting after work tomorrow loves it."

Five

Mud wrestling.

Nick laughed softly as he pulled on a pair of jeans.

Mud wrestling.

He laughed again, remembering. He tucked in the T-shirt he'd put on earlier, zipped up the jeans, then sat down on the edge of his bed and began to put on a pair of motorcycle boots.

Okay, he admitted to himself. Maybe it *had* been a tad extreme for the second installment of "Operation: Mr. Wrong." But Hayley had risen—or was it sunk?—to the challenge just as he'd expected she would. She'd handled Michael "The Mickster" Becker and his passion for down-and-dirty athletic events perfectly. What's more, he was ready to swear in court that she'd had a good time doing it.

Her performance two nights later had been entirely different but no less terrific. On the agenda: Ninety minutes of self-centered psycho-babble from Michael "I'm Totally in Touch with My Feelings" Becker. He'd pushed the character to the outer edge of parody. Hayley had pushed right back with some of the wickedest one-liners he'd heard in a long time.

Neither The Mickster nor Mr. Feelings had tried to kiss Hayley at the end of their respective evenings together. The former had been too busy panting over the "fabulous gazongas" on his favorite mud wrestler to pucker up. The latter had excused himself on grounds that he had a deep-seated fear of intimacy.

As for the man who'd been playing both parts...

Nick stopped laughing and stood up.

No. He hadn't tried to kiss Hayley, either. Not again. Not...yet. Not until he'd come to terms with the storm of emotion that had erupted inside him the first time he'd claimed her lips with his own.

Five days had gone by since that kiss. Five days, and he was still asking himself whether what he'd experienced with Hayley had been too much, not enough, or some mind-blowing mixture of both. He had no way of judging the matter at this point. All his previous standards of comparison seemed to have been obliterated.

Nick was hooked and he knew it. He was hooked in a way he'd never been hooked before and, to his astonishment, he felt no urge to break loose.

The attraction Hayley held for him wasn't just sexual. Yes, he desired her physically. All he had to do was think about the way she'd looked in that red satin lingerie and his blood turned hot and his body went hard.

He'd wanted her before that inebriated episode in her bedroom, too.

The sunshine-silk of her hair.

The sweet scent of her skin.

The sultry shape of her mouth.

Those things had fueled his fantasies for months. But there was more than that. Much more.

To put it simply: Nick O'Neill had discovered that Hayley Jerome was a bigger con artist than he was and it entranced him. He wanted to chart and cherish every kink and quirk in her personality. He wanted to know Hayley intimately. Absolutely. And he wanted her to know him in the same way.

But before any of that could happen, he had to understand why she was so determined to disguise—no, worse—to *deny* the qualities that made her so special. He also had to find out why she could be free with him when he was pretending to be Michael Becker but froze up whenever he reverted to being himself.

Nick leaned over and snagged the leather jacket he'd tossed across the foot of his bed a short time before. He shrugged into the garment, then crossed to the full-length mirror that hung on the back of his bedroom door.

"What are you so afraid of, Hayley?" he'd asked in a whisper five days before.

"N-nothing," she'd responded, the tremor in her voice making a lie of her answer. *"I'm not afraid of anything."*

"Yes, you are," he'd contradicted, touching the corners of the ripe and rosy mouth he'd intended to kiss. *"The only question is whether you're afraid of me . . . or yourself . . . or both of us together."*

Nick rubbed his beard-stubbled chin and scrutinized his reflection.

He'd been wrong five days before. There were a hell of a lot more questions than the one he'd put to Hayley. Besides, he already knew the answer to that particular inquiry. It was All of the Above. Hayley was afraid of herself. And him. And the two of them together.

Next question.

Why?

Maybe . . . just maybe . . . he'd figured out a way to find out. Or, at the very least, to make a start at finding out.

Nick narrowed his eyes, still assessing his mirrored image.

The leather jacket. Black and battered.

The T-shirt. White and tight.

The jeans. Even tighter.

The boots. Scuffed but made to swagger.

Nick nodded his approval.

He hadn't worn this gear for more than six months. The last time he'd had it on had been the day he'd wrapped up a baby-sitting assignment involving a federally protected witness. He'd been in the midst of typing up his report when Al Kozlow had walked in with a blue-eyed blonde who'd made every male instinct he had stir to attention.

"Jerome, meet O'Neill. Don't be fooled by his appearance. He's worse than he looks," Al had rumbled. *"O'Neill, meet Jerome. Get to know each other."*

Hayley examined herself in the mirror that hung over her bathroom sink. She made a minute adjustment to the neckline of the white angora sweater she had on. The garment was something she'd seen on sale, purchased on impulse, then regretted buying when she'd gotten home. It had been sitting in her drawer for more than three months. She'd briefly considered wearing it into the office on an unseasonable chilly day several weeks before but had soon rejected the idea. Frivolous fripperies were not part of her on-the-job style.

If they could see me now, she thought with a sudden hint of mischief, conjuring up mental images of several of her colleagues. Then she flushed.

No, she amended swiftly. God forbid that anyone she knew—much less worked with—should see her looking like this. Anyone, that is, except Ni—er, Michael.

Hayley grimaced slightly and went back to studying her reflection.

Not bad, she decided after several seconds, licking a smudge of hot pink lipstick off her front teeth. Not bad at all.

She glanced at her wristwatch, the armload of bangle bracelets she'd piled on earlier clicking noisily. It was almost eleven. Ni—er, Michael should be calling for her any minute.

No. Wait. Not Michael. Mikey. The character who'd left a message on her answering machine the previous evening had called himself Mikey.

"Hey, 'beep' to you, too," he'd begun. *"Yo, Hayley. It's me, babe. Mikey. Mikey Becker. Your one and only. At least I bettuh be your one and only. So, anyway, babe. Why I called. Tomorruh. Saddiday. I pick you up at 'leven. Buy you a little lunch in my old neighborhood. Maybe take you to a movie. That's 'leven a.m. Don' keep me waitin'."*

And then he'd hung up.

Hayley shook her head again.

"Mikey" Becker.

Nick obviously intended to play this latest entry in the Mr. Wrong sweepstakes to the hilt. She'd heard the grin in his voice throughout the message he'd left. He was planning on having a ball.

Which was fine with her. Because she was looking forward to indulging in a little game-playing, too. She expected that her encounter with Mikey was going to be at least as much fun as her interludes with the Mickster and Michael "I'm So Sensitive" Becker.

The past seven days had been among the most unsettling of her life. Which was saying a lot, considering her history. Yet those same seven days had also been the most exhilarating she'd ever experienced. There were times when she had no idea what she was doing. She only knew that—to judge by Nick's reactions—she was doing it very well.

Hayley blinked suddenly.

Nick's reactions.

She smoothed her right palm slowly down the front of the pencil-slim skirt she was wearing. Then she frowned.

Nick's reactions?

God. What was happening to her? Was she actually starting to measure herself by the standards of a man who brazenly admitted that his mission in life was to scam people? Was she crazy? How could she be sure that his reactions to anything, including her, were real? Didn't she realize that it was entirely possible he was deceiving her into believing that she was capable of carrying off their con when she wasn't?

But . . . why would Nick want to do that? she asked herself.

Hayley bit her lip. She looked at her reflection again. She saw the teased hair. The glossy lipstick. The provocatively soft sweater.

An angry, inarticulate sound broke from her throat. She whirled away from the mirror and stormed out of the bathroom.

How was she supposed to know why he'd want to do that? she fumed silently. She couldn't read his mind! At least not—oh, all right. All right! All right! There *had* been times this past week when she tuned in to the pattern of Nick's thoughts. Times when she'd sensed what he was going to do or say before he did or said it. But it hadn't been a constant or consistent thing. For every moment Nicholas James O'Neill's methods and motives had seemed as transparent as crystal to her, there'd been a dozen more when they were as opaque as a lead-lined brick wall.

Hayley came to a halt in the middle of her serene blue and ivory living room. Her breath was going in and out in quick little snatches.

She still hadn't figured out why Nick had invited her to dinner and encouraged her to get drunk. Nor had she been able to come to any firm conclusions about why he was participating in "Operation: Mr. Wrong" with such enthusiasm.

She also had no idea what had prompted him to kiss her so passionately five days before. And she was damned if she knew why he hadn't offered her so much as a chaste peck on the cheek—

Hayley slammed the brakes on this train of thought. After a moment she realized she'd lifted her right hand to touch her mouth. Her lips were trembling. She pressed them together and forced herself to lower her arm.

She did not—repeat, with emphasis—did *not* want Nick to kiss her again. She hadn't wanted him to kiss her in the first place! Or, if she had, it hadn't been a rational kind of wanting. It had been the kind of wanting that was part relief over the fact that he hadn't been knifed to death, part rage that he'd taken such a stupid risk, and part... part...

Buzzzzzz.

Hayley started at the summons from her security intercom. She hesitated for a few moments, then stalked over to the small speaker set into the left wall of her foyer.

Buzzzzzz.

She thumbed the proper switch. "Hello?"

"Yo, babe. It's me, Mikey. You ready to rock and roll?"

Hayley wasn't, but she went anyway.

Their waitress's name was Candie Crandall and Hayley decided it was a testament to something—silcone, maybe?—that her brassiere cups didn't overflow every time she bent and placed something in front of "Mikey Becker."

"Such service," she muttered as she watched Candie sashay away from their table for the fifth time.

Nick suppressed a grin. Although he found Ms. Crandall's overblown charms supremely resistible, he appreciated the effect they were having on Hayley. To say that his lunch date had not reacted well to his choice of wardrobe was an understatement. It had taken nearly ninety minutes, but something had finally put a crack in her Ice Princess facade.

"Such scenery," he responded with a leer.

Hayley hammered him with a look. "Let me guess, Mikey. You visited the Grand Canyon at the same time you were going through puberty and you never got over it."

Maintaining his Mikey character, Nick reacted as though he'd just been accused of some kind of perversion.

"Hey—" he gestured with both hands "—I got over puberty just fine, thank you very much. I mean—" more gesturing "—does this look like the physique of an adolescent? No, babe. I think not. I definitely think not."

Hayley stared at him. At the powerful, leather-clad shoulders. At the taut, T-shirted torso. Her mind's eye provided some very explicit reminders about the part of him she couldn't see at the moment.

No, she reflected, shifting in her seat and crossing her legs well above the knee. His was definitely not the physique of an adolescent. It wasn't even the physique of the average

American man. The average American man would kill to have Nick O'Neill's body.

To say nothing of what the average American woman might do.

Hayley felt herself flush. She lowered her gaze, acutely conscious that Nick—not Mikey—was watching her very intently.

"It's not like I'm flauntin' myself," Nick went on, feigning an air of injured innocence.

Hayley's head snapped up. "Oh, please!" she retorted.

If he wasn't flaunting, then she was a frozen fish stick. And he was doing it on purpose, too. She could tell. Somehow, someway, he'd figured out the impact he'd had on her the first time they'd met.

"What can I tell you, babe?" he asked, then sighed heavily. "It's my natural animal magnitude. I try, but I can't control it."

Once before, Nick had brought Hayley to the brink of losing her temper only to defuse her anger by making her laugh. She tried to hold back this time just as she had the first. She truly did. But she simply couldn't.

"N-natural...animal...*m-magnitude?*" she spluttered helplessly. "Is *that* what you h-have?"

Nick grinned, shedding all of Mikey's mannerisms. He retained the accent long enough to crack, "Wha'didja think it was? Some kinda sociable disease?"

That set Hayley off again. She laughed until she was giddy from lack of oxygen. "N-no more," she pleaded faintly. "Please."

Nick let about a minute go by. This gave Hayley sufficient time to recover her ability to breath normally but nowhere near enough to rebuild the defenses that had just come tumbling down. He leaned forward.

"It bothers you, doesn't it?" he asked quietly.

Hayley paused in the act of bringing a glass of water to her lips. Her first impulse was to parry the question with a joke. But while the inquiry was oblique, the expression she saw in Nick's eyes was not. It was very, very direct. She slowly set down the glass.

"What?" she returned after a few seconds.

"The way I look today. The way I looked the first time we met."

Hayley swallowed. Her mouth was dry. So was her throat. "Well, it's a little...disconcerting, Nick," she acknowledged awkwardly.

"Mmm." He forked one hand back through his dark hair. "Do you think this is the real me?"

The question startled her. "No!" The response was quick and sharp. What followed was slower and had all the edges rounded off. "No...of course not."

Nick considered this for a moment or two, then went at his target from a different direction. "I'll bet I know what was going through your head when we were introduced."

Hayley felt her heart skip a beat. "I'll bet you don't," she responded. Her tone was bantering but brittle.

Nick stiffened. There it was again in her eyes. That damned flash of fear! Didn't she realize he'd never do anything to hurt her? Didn't she know she could trust him?

Maybe she did. Maybe she didn't.

Part of him wanted to push. To probe. To dig down to the essence of this woman he found so fascinating. He didn't doubt for an instant that he could manipulate Hayley into telling him what he wanted to know. Lord knew, he'd had a lifetime's worth of lessons in twisting people to his own ends.

But he couldn't use those lessons on Hayley. Not anymore. She'd never forgive him if he did. He'd never forgive himself, either.

"Nick?" Hayley asked uncertainly, trying to make sense of the emotions she saw flickering across his mobile face.

Nick forced himself to relax his posture and to unclench his hands. Then he forced himself to smile. "I'll bet you thought things must be pretty bad if the Justice Department was hiring common hoodlums," he said lightly.

He saw her eyes widen. Heard her exhale suddenly, as though she'd been holding her breath. Sensed her testing each one of his words for hidden meanings and half-truths.

And then, after an unknowable amount of time, he watched her return his smile.

"I may have thought things were pretty bad, Nick," she responded. "But I never thought you were common."

Candie sauntered over with their lunch orders a few moments later. Once she left, they settled down to eat.

Their conversation was casual—at least on the surface— throughout most of the meal. They spoke mainly about work. It wasn't until they were finishing up that Nick very deliberately brought up a very personal topic.

"So, Hayley," he began, dragging a French fry through the pool of ketchup he'd poured on his plate. "Tell me about your mother."

Hayley dabbed at her mouth with a paper napkin. "My mother?" she echoed, suddenly wary.

Nick ate the condiment-coated potato in two quick bites. "I'm going to be meeting her, right?"

"Ah—"

"As Michael Becker," he amended quickly. "I'm going to meet her as Michael Becker."

"Oh." She crumpled the napkin and dropped it on the table. "Yes."

"Well, it would help me if I knew a little more about her. I still haven't figured out which Mr. Wrong is going to be right."

"Definitely *not* Mikey Becker." The response just slipped out.

Nick raised his brows, wordlessly inviting her to elaborate.

Hayley manufactured a laugh. "Too much natural animal magnitude," she quipped, wishing she'd watched her tongue.

Nick reverted to character. "Your old lady's a real hot numbuh, huh?"

He said it jokingly, but Hayley knew that the core of the question was serious. She hesitated for a few seconds, then countered carefully, "What makes you think that?"

"You mean, aside from her taste in your underwear?"

It was the first time Nick had mentioned what he'd seen eight nights before. He was aware he was taking a chance in bringing up the matter, but he wanted to know about that red-hot satin lingerie. To his way of thinking, that sizzlingly seductive underwear was a metaphor for all the qualities Hayley tried so hard to keep so hidden.

Hayley flushed but managed to meet his gaze steadily. She didn't pretend not to understand his reference. "I...told you she'd sent—?"

"For Michael."

"Oh." She felt the hot color in her cheeks intensify. She studied Nick's expression. It was obvious he was debating something with himself. "What?" she finally asked.

Nick's mouth twisted. "I've got a question that will probably get my face slapped," he confessed. "But, uh—" he cleared his throat "—I may go nuts if I don't ask it."

An odd little thrill danced up Hayley's spine. After a brief silence, she folded her hands and placed them on the table. "Ask."

"Had you ever worn that underwear before? To work, I mean."

Now it was her turn to clear her throat. "No."

"Was there any special reason—?"

Hayley grimaced. "I hadn't had time to do laundry."

"Huh?"

"I'd been putting in a lot of extra hours at the office and my schedule at home was thrown off. I usually do my washing on Thursday night. But I didn't get around to it last week. I needed something clean and...well..." Unfolding her hands, she gestured. Then she added a bit stiffly, "Anyway, I don't like to let things go to waste, Nick. It—the red, uh—it had been sitting in my drawer for weeks."

"I see." Nick studied her for several seconds. He was suddenly tempted to ask her about the white angora sweater she was wearing. He was sure he'd never seen it before. Lord knew, he would have remembered if he had! How long had *it* been sitting around in a drawer? he wondered. Was it, too, a gift from her mother? Or did the Hayley who leavened her extensive collection of serious books with fairy tales and romances also spice her wardrobe of tailored suits and de-mure dresses with subtly sexy fluff?

"I'm not wearing it now, if that's what you're think-ing," Hayley said, suddenly very conscious of the way the clothes she had on were clinging to her body. She'd chosen her outfit to match the man she'd envisioned from the mes-sage left on her machine. Maybe she'd gone a bit too far.

Nick's mouth quirked. "I didn't figure Mikey'd get that lucky." He decided to shelve the subject of the sweater. There were more important topics to pursue. "But—let's get back to your mother. What's she like?"

"You talked to her on the telephone. What do you think?" There was an element of evasion in this response and Hayley knew it. She also knew that she was genuinely curious to hear how Nick would answer.

"She's . . . different," he said.

"From me."

He made a noncommittal sound.

"You think I'm like her?"

Careful, Nick warned himself. "I can't answer that."

"Can't or won't?"

"Can't. At least, not yet. You tell me what you think she's like, and I'll tell you whether I think you're like her."

Hayley eyed him consideringly. "I'll bet you can't say that last sentence over again and get it straight."

Nick chuckled. "I'll bet you're right. Now, come on."

Hayley picked up the paper napkin she'd put down a few minutes before and began to fiddle with it. "I love my mother, Nick," she said finally.

"I know that."

"She's a wonderful woman."

"So you've said."

"When did I—oh. Then."

"Yes, then. Go on."

Hayley sighed. "My mother is—is—" She shredded the napkin, searching for the right words. "My mother is a hu-man earthquake."

Nick kept his expression neutral. "Destructive?"

"No. Oh, no," came the quick and convincing response. Then, after a tiny pause, Hayley reluctantly added, "At least, not on purpose. My mother is just...well, she has this *mania* for shaking things up."

Especially her daughter, Nick added silently.

"In other words, she likes to rearrange the landscape of life," he said aloud, earning a sweetly rueful smile.

"Something like that," Hayley agreed. "She loves change, and she's got more than enough money to indulge her whims. She also has a very limited attention span."

"She gets bored."

"She loses interest."

"But not in you." It wasn't really a question.

"No. Not in me." Hayley gave Nick another smile. She was aware that she was telling him things she'd never told anyone else. She was also aware that it felt right to do so.

"Did you ever wish she would?" he asked slowly. "Lose interest in you, I mean."

Hayley opened her fingers. Bits and pieces of napkin fluttered onto the table like confetti. "Sometimes," she admitted. "I—I know it sounds awful. But it can be very unsettling being the focus of my mother's attention."

"Unsettling?"

"Yes. Unsettling. I realize I've been lucky in a lot of ways, Nick. I've never lacked for anything except, well, I guess 'stability' is as good a word as any. But not having that one thing has made me—oh, I don't know! What I do know is that the longest I've ever lived in the same place is thirteen months. I've had four stepfathers. I've spent time in at least twenty different states, and I've been around the world two—no, *three*—times. Not including college—which I paid for myself—I've attended fourteen different schools. I've had lessons in everything from cordon bleu cooking to karate. I've lived with baroque, Biedermeier, Bauhaus, and everything in between. When I was eight, I went to camp for a week. One week. When I got home, my mother had had my bedroom completely redecorated." She shook her head. "What can I say? It was a surprise. One of many."

Nick remained silent for nearly thirty seconds, absorbing what he'd just heard. God. No wonder Hayley tried to deny her own impulses and urges. No wonder she professed to abhor the unexpected. No wonder she couldn't allow herself to accept the idea that there might be a middle ground between absolute control and constant upheaval...a middle ground where he knew she would blossom as she was meant to.

"What kind of redecoration job did she do?" he asked eventually.

Hayley blinked, genuinely thrown by the question. "I—I don't remem—" she began, then broke off abruptly.

No. That was a lie. She remembered. She remembered the room and her first horrified reaction to it. She also remembered that once she'd recovered from the frightening sense of loss—from the shocked realization that the haven she'd so carefully organized had been snatched away—she'd adapted to her new surroundings with remarkable speed.

"Hayley?"

She heard concern in his voice, saw it in his gray-green eyes. She smiled, just a little, to tell him she was all right.

"She had the walls and ceiling done in a beautiful blue. Like the sky," Hayley said. "She even had some clouds painted in. There was a chaise longue covered with velvet. And a huge four-poster bed with a canopy. The cover was trimmed with ribbons and embroidered with stars. The room was...beautiful."

"But it wasn't yours."

"No. Not at first."

"And once it was, your mother redecorated again?"

Hayley shook her head. "And once it was, she married Dr. Eduardo Martinez de la Madrid and we moved to Washington."

Six

"**I** was not."

"You were, too."

"No way."

"You were sniveling all through the last scene of the movie."

"*Sniveling?*"

"I know a snivel when I hear one, Nick."

"Considering the way *you* were carrying on, Hayley, I'm amazed you could hear anything—much less a single, solitary snivel."

"Ah-ha! Then you admit it."

"Admit what?"

"That you were sniveling all through the last scene of the movie."

Nick grinned and reached for Hayley's hand. "Actually, it was all through the last reel."

Hayley laughed and let her fingers lace with his. "Me, too," she confessed.

It was now late in the afternoon. The sun was sinking in the west, shadows were growing long. The autumn air had acquired an invigorating nippiness.

About three hours had passed since Hayley had let down her guard and told Nick some of the things he wanted to know about her. How much more she would have told him had Candie Crandall not come bouncing back to their table, Nick could never be sure.

He hadn't tried to pick up the thread of their conversation once the waitress had departed to total their bill. He'd told himself that was up to Hayley to do. Although he'd experienced a pang of frustration when she'd chosen to introduce an impersonal topic, he hadn't rejected it.

After he'd paid the tab—"Keep the change, it's been a pleasure," he'd told Candie. "Keep the check, it's got my number," she'd responded—Hayley had reminded him about the message he'd left on her answering machine. After a bit of strolling around, they'd found a movie both of them wanted to see.

"Do you think Mickey Becker would have enjoyed that picture?" Hayley queried, slanting Nick a teasing look.

"What? With no Stallone? No Schwarzenegger? No chainsaw—" Nick broke off suddenly, checking himself in midstride.

Hayley came to a halt as well. "Nick? What's the—"

He silenced her with a quick gesture. They were standing in front of the entrance to a shadowed alley. He cocked his head, obviously listening for something.

Hayley listened, too. For what she had no idea. And then, suddenly, she heard it.

The sound was muffled but unmistakable. It was sobbing. Helpless, heartbroken sobbing, coming from the alley.

Blue eyes met hazel ones.

"Let's go check it out," Nick said grimly.

The source of the sobbing was a small, brown-haired boy. Nick and Hayley found him huddled under a fire escape, half hidden by a stack of discarded cardboard cartons.

"Oh, no!" Hayley's immediate impulse was to rush to the child and offer any help she could. But Nick caught her by the arm as she started to move forward and motioned for her to stay put.

In the same instant, the child lifted his head. His face was freckled and contorted with anguish. His cheeks were blotched and smudged with filth. His nose was red and running. The feathery lashes of his big brown eyes were spangled with tears.

Despite his distressed condition, it was obvious the youngster was no street urchin. His clothing—a bright red sweatshirt and blue jeans—was a bit dirty but looked fairly new. The sneakers on his small feet were an expensive brand endorsed by many athletes. And while his toffee-colored hair was wildly tousled, it had a healthy sheen.

"I didn't mean to!" he cried, gazing up at them with a stricken expression. "I only wanted to go to play v-video games. Charlie *n-never* takes me w-with him when he g-goes. But today Mom said he had to. 'Cept as soon as we got part way there, Charlie called me a b-bratty booger brain and runned away. And I r-runned after him and y-yelled for him to stop but he d-didn't. So I runned more. Only... only pretty soon I couldn't see him. And then I looked around and I d-didn't know where I was. And there was this—this me-mean lady who who l-looked like a witch with icky t-teeth and I 'membered Charlie once told me there are r-really-truly witches who eat you up even if grown-ups say th-there aren't. And... and I started to get sc-scared so I runned more to get away. Only I g-guess I didn't look where I was going g-good enough, 'cuz a car n-nearly squished m-me. And then I b-bumped into this fruit man and made h-his apples fall on the ground. And he y-yelled at m-me really loud. I think—I *think* he was y-yelling I w-was bad and tried to take his apples. Only I didn't! But I was scared the p-police would c-come and b'lieve him and arrest me and p-put me in jail. Charlie says... he says there are giant *r-rats* in there. In jail. So... so I runned and I hided in h-here. Only... only I d-don't know where h-h-here is and I think... I think I'm r-really l-l-lost!"

The child's litany of woes got shriller as it poured out of him. By the last sentence, he was obviously teetering on the brink of hysteria. It was Nick who pulled him back.

"Sounds like you've had a tough day, buddy," he observed in a matter-of-fact voice once the little boy finally stopped speaking.

Hayley gaped at Nick, appalled by his apparent insensitivity. What in the name of heaven was he thinking? she wondered angrily. This poor child needed to be cuddled and cosseted, not casually told he'd had a tough day!

At least she *thought* that was what he needed. To her astonishment, the "poor child" seemed comforted by Nick's offhand comment.

"Y-yeah," the youngster responded after a few seconds. Although his voice caught pathetically on the affirmative, his tone was infinitely calmer than the last time he'd spoken. "Really t-tough."

Nick took an easy, ambling step forward. "I'll bet Charlie couldn't handle such a tough day."

The little boy considered this. His lower lip quivered for an instant, then steadied up. "Probably he c-couldn't," he agreed.

Nick took another step forward, his posture relaxed, his expression open and benign. He might be dressed like a hoodlum, but he was radiating more reassurance than Mr. Rogers. Hayley watched him move toward the child, her outrage of less than a minute before dissolving in a sense of wonder. Was there no end to this man's ability to transform his personality?

"Is he your brother?" Nick asked.

"Charlie?"

"Uh-huh."

"Y-yeah. Do you . . . do you know him?"

Nick shook his head, taking the step that put him within touching distance of the little boy. He hunkered down with coiled-spring athleticism, bringing himself to the child's eye level. He let his hands dangle between his knees, making no effort to reach out and establish physical contact.

"No, I don't know Charlie," he admitted. "And, to tell you the truth, buddy, I'm not sure I want to. It sounds to me like *he's* the bratty—uh—boogie brain, not you."

The child made a sound that was half-choke, half-giggle. "Not *boogie* brain," he corrected. "Booger."

"Ah. Sorry."

There was a brief pause as the youngster sniffed loudly, then dragged the back of his grubby right hand beneath his equally grubby nose. "Charlie's even a worser thing than that. Only I can't say it 'cuz it's a b-bad word."

"Oh, really? And just where did you hear this bad word?"

"From Charlie."

Hayley had to swallow a sudden laugh. She began to edge closer, trying to keep her approach as unthreatening as Nick's had been.

"No kidding." Nick sounded genuinely interested in the matter.

"Yeah. He tells it in my ear so nobody can hear him. He says if I tell, Mom will wash my mouth out with soap. He says he'll pound me, too."

"Oh, he's *definitely* worse than a bratty booger brain. I'd better be on the look-out for him. What's his whole name?"

"Charles Andrew Ross."

"Charles Andrew Ross," Nick repeated. "My whole name is Nicholas James O'Neill. But people call me Nick. What do people call you?"

It almost worked. Hayley watched the little boy start to open his mouth, then shut it abruptly. She winced as she saw a look of anxiety cloud his soft brown eyes.

"I'm n-not s'posed to tell my name to strangers," the child declared, hunching into himself. He sniffed. "It's a r-rule."

"That's a very smart rule," Nick responded gravely, showing no hint of the frustration Hayley knew he must be feeling.

"I'm not s'posed to take c-c-candy or rides from them, neither. Strangers s-sometimes do bad things."

"Yeah. Sometimes they do, buddy."

"Are you—" the eyes staring up at Nick were opened so widely that the whites showed all the way around the brown irises "—going to do b-bad things?"

The tremulous question made Hayley's heart ache. Moving next to Nick, she knelt down. "Oh, no, sweetie," she said, shaking her head. "No. Never. We just want to help you."

The little boy's gaze ping-ponged between her and Nick for several moments. Finally he relaxed a bit and confided, "My mommy calls me that."

"What?" Hayley repressed an urge to reach out and stroke the child's mussed-up hair. She was certain an attempt to touch would spook, not soothe. Out of the corner of her eye, she caught a barely perceptible nod of approval from Nick. "Sweetie?"

"Y-yeah. When she kisses me g'night." The youngster gnawed his lower lip for several moments, his forehead furrowing. Finally he asked in a forlorn voice, "She's gonna be really m-mad at me, huh?"

"Probably," Nick acknowledged. Hayley suddenly realized that the reason he was doing so well with the little boy was that he wasn't talking down to him. Most adults—herself included—would have responded to the child's last question with a sugar-coated lie. A lie the child undoubtedly would have detected. But Nick was being honest. And in being honest, he was earning trust.

"She m-might even spank me."

"Mmm, maybe. Then again, she might be so glad to see you that she forgets all about being angry."

"You think?"

"Uh-huh."

"But... but how can she see me if I d-don't know where I am?"

"You could let us help you," Hayley told him.

"You mean, you could bring me h-home?"

"If you want us to."

"Would I have to take a r-ride from you?" The question was nervous.

"We don't have a car," Nick told him. "We came here on the subway."

"Oh." The child chewed his lip for several seconds, his eyes moving back and forth. Finally his gaze settled on Nick. "I—I don't 'member your name."

"Nick. Nick O'Neill."

"Nick." The child repeated.

"And I'm Hayley."

"Hayley... O'Neill?"

Hayley felt her pulse stutter for an instant. She waited for it to recover its usual rhythm, then gently corrected, "Hayley Jerome."

"Oh."

More lip chewing, more eye shifting.

"Can you read, buddy?" Nick asked after a few moments.

The little boy looked startled. Hayley understood his reaction. The question struck her as extremely strange, too.

"I know the alphabet from *Sesame Street,*" the child answered.

"That's good. Very good."

"But I can't read yet. I'm only in kindergarten."

"Hey, no problem. If you know the alphabet, we're in terrific shape." Nick winked at the child, then became serious. "Now, I want to take something out of my pocket and show it to you," he declared. "And once you check it out, maybe you'll tell us your name and we can help you get home. Okay?"

The youngster glanced at Hayley, clearly uncertain. She smiled encouragingly. She didn't have a clue about what Nick intended to do, but she was willing to play along with it.

The little boy transferred his gaze back to Nick, then bobbed his head. "Okay... Nick," he agreed.

"All right. I'll do this nice and carefully for you." Matching action to words, Nick reached slowly into the right rear pocket of his jeans and extracted his wallet. He opened it and took out an identification card.

Although the light in the alley was fading fast, there was enough illumination for Hayley to make out what was printed and embossed on the impressive-looking ID. She nearly choked on the implications of what she was seeing. Merciful heaven! How had Nick gotten hold of one of *those?*

"Here we go," he said, presenting the plastic card to the little boy.

The youngster took the item in both hands and scrutinized it for several tense moments. He looked from the card to Nick and back again.

"This is you!" he exclaimed. "This picture shows you, Nick!"

"Good eye, buddy," Nick congratulated him. "Now, can you read those three letters there at the top? The big ones?"

The child studied the card again, his forehead wrinkling. Finally he named each letter aloud. Then he raised his eyes to Nick's once more. His mouth was hanging open. His expression was awed.

"Are you—are you an...*agent?*" he breathed.

"You've got the ID badge right there," Nick answered. "What do you think?"

"You are! You are!" came the excited response. The little boy clutched the ID card to his sweatshirted chest. "Wow. Oh, wow. Wait till I tell Charlie!"

"You have to get home before you tell Charlie," Hayley pointed out softly. While she certainly couldn't endorse conning an innocent child, she was willing to acquiesce to the scam if it achieved the desired objective.

The youngster blinked. "Oh, yeah," he agreed, nodding his head. He wiped his nose with the cuff of his right sleeve. Then he took a deep breath and recited an address and telephone number. The information came out in a rush. After pausing to draw another breath, he concluded brightly, "And my real name is Michael Lawrence Ross. Everybody calls me Mikey."

"So," Nick murmured, tracing the curve of Hayley's cheek with the tip of one finger, "are you going to squeal on me?"

"You mean, am I going to report you to the proper authorities for illegally impersonating an agent?" she countered, brushing her hand against his well-worn leather jacket.

"Mmm."

"Well, seeing that I was an accomplice to your impersonation, I'd have to incriminate myself to incriminate you."

"Cop a plea and rat me out." He thrust his hands into his pockets.

She pretended to consider this, then shook her head.

They were standing in front of Hayley's apartment building. It was nearly eight p.m. Mikey had been safely restored to his family about two hours before. The reunion had been an emotional one. While the little boy's parents had clearly found Nick's appearance unnerving at first, they'd calmed down after he'd opened his wallet and flashed an ID card. His *legitimate* ID card, Hayley had been relieved to note.

She'd also noted that the same badge had made quite an impression on Charlie Ross. Before she and Nick left, he'd sworn he would take his younger brother to play video games every single Saturday for the rest of their lives. He'd even offered to give Mikey half of his superhero action figures. Mikey had turned up his freckled nose at the latter, scornfully informing his sibling that he had no need of 'pretend' superheroes since he personally knew a real-life government agent.

Hayley smiled a little at the memory. "That fake ID of yours was very effective," she commented.

Nick regarded her silently for several moments, then asked, "What makes you think it was fake?"

"Because you're not—" she began automatically, then broke off with gasp. *"Nick!* Oh, God. You *aren't!"*

He let her stew in the juices of her own imaginative speculations for several seconds, then grinned. "No, I 'aren't.'"

Hayley gave him a nasty look. "Why you—you—"

"Booger brain?" he suggested helpfully.

"Con artist," she retorted.

He shrugged. "Yes, well, I warned you about that."

Hayley grimaced. She supposed he had. "Exactly where *did* you get that ID?"

"From a friend."

"You must have extremely interesting friends."

"A few of them are marginally respectable, too."

"I'll have to reserve judgment on that."

Nick chuckled. "You really want to know about the ID?"

"Yes. Really."

"Okay." He paused for a moment, apparently considering how much he wanted to say. Pulling his hands out of his pockets, he forked his fingers back through his hair. Then he began.

"A few years back I was working undercover on an arms smuggling case and I stumbled into a covert operation," he said flatly. "It was basically another instance where the government's right hand didn't know what the government's left hand was doing. One of the good guys involved was somebody I'd met early in my career. We'd both had to do some closed door testifying on Capitol Hill. Anyway, he decided that since I already had mud on my shoes, I might as well go down and dirty. To make a long story short, we pretty much got the job done. One snake managed to slither off into the night, but we skinned the rest. After it was all over, my old buddy had the ID made up for me. A memento of a rare moment of interagency cooperation, he said. It looks real until you start reading the fine print."

"Which very few people do," Hayley surmised. Instinct told her not to push for details about the covert operation or the "snakes."

"Which very few people do," he agreed.

"It certainly did the trick with Mikey."

"Good thing." Nick grinned. "Five-year-olds are tough. They may take Santa Claus on trust, but that's about it."

She smiled, recalling the sense of wonder she'd experienced as she'd watched Nick interacting with Mikey. He'd shown such . . . kindness. Such compassion. He'd been perfectly attuned to the little boy's needs.

"You were terrific today, Nick," she said softly.

He raised his brows. "Surprised you, right?"

Hayley wasn't certain whether he was mocking her or himself. Either way, his words flicked her on a raw spot she hadn't realized she had.

"No," she denied swiftly, sincerely. Then she paused, her emotions suddenly jumbled. She stared up at Nick, trying to make sense of the feelings roiling around inside her. She opened her mouth to speak, then closed it again. She realized she wasn't sure of what she wanted to say, much less of how she wanted to say it.

"Hayley?" Nick prompted after a moment. He wasn't mocking either one of them anymore.

"It's just that—" she gestured, wishing she could pluck the right words out of the air. "Well... it's getting to the point where *nothing* you do surprises me."

Silence.

Nick went very still. His features coalesced into an angular, unreadable mask. Only his hazel eyes moved, shifting back and forth. Finally he exhaled on a long whistle.

"Hayley...Hayley..." he said, seeming to taste her name as he spoke it. "You shouldn't give somebody like me an opening like that."

"Why not?" A strange kind of anticipation sparked to life within her. It licked at her like a flame, offering both warmth and warning.

"Because I might take advantage of it, angel."

The endearment jolted her. She suddenly remembered he'd used it once before, when she'd nearly passed out in her living room after he'd nonchalantly referred to taking off her clothes. She lifted her chin slightly.

"Really?" she asked.

He nodded once. "Really."

"What... kind of advantage?"

His gaze dipped from her eyes to her lips and back again. "Any kind I can."

Hayley swallowed. It wasn't easy. Her throat had gone as dry as dust. "It sounds like it might be...fun," she said after several breathless moments.

Nick lifted both his hands and gently cupped her face. She quivered a little as his palms curved against her jaw and his fingers teased the lobes of her ears. "It might be a lot more than that," he told her.

Then he dipped his head. Hayley closed her eyes.

Their breaths married. Their mouths met and mated.

Tender... yet strangely tentative. Those qualities defined the kiss more than any other. There was heat and hunger, too. Yet throughout the caress, Hayley sensed Nick was holding back.

"Nick," she said on a shaky sigh when he finally released her. There was a knot in her stomach and an ache lower down. She was trembling.

"I know," he answered, not bothering to elaborate. Dipping his head again, he brushed his lips briefly against hers. Then he jammed his hands into his pockets again and took a step back.

Hayley stared at him, confused. She whispered his name again and saw him shake his head.

"Look," he said, his voice husky. "I've got to go out of town for a couple of days."

"Out of town?" she repeated blankly.

"Yeah. My mother's discovered I'm on vacation, and she expects a visit. If I don't go willingly, Deke will show up and drag me."

"How—" she swallowed "—how l-long?"

"I'll be back Thursday morning. I'll take you to lunch."

Hayley blinked. "You?" she echoed. "Or...Michael Becker?"

Nick's sensually shaped mouth tightened for a second, then relaxed into a crooked smile. "Michael, of course. And watch out for this one. He's kind of kinky."

"Kind of kinky" didn't begin to describe the man Hayley met for lunch on Thursday. She wasn't surprised to discover this. She'd had a feeling—a hunch—that Nick might have erred on the side of understatement when he'd characterized his fifth entry in the Mr. Wrong sweepstakes. So, she'd come prepared.

And when her preparations had proven less than adequate, she'd improvised.

"Extension 2976."

"I ought to put you over my knee, you little witch."

"Oh, my. I'm afraid you must have misdialed, sir. I think you want one of those 900 numbers. You know. The kind that advertises on late night television? Have you tried 1-900-E-Z—"

"Just tell me what you do with the peanut butter."

"Any man who talks about making home videos featuring eggplants, Doberman pinschers, and people in skin diving suits should be able to figure out what to do with a jar of peanut butter."

"A jar? You use a *jar* of the stuff?"

"Mmm . . . that depends."

"On what?"

"On whether it's creamy or crunchy."

"Did anyone ever tell you that you're warped?"

"Is that better or worse than kind of kinky?"

"Worse. Much worse."

"Oh, goodie."

A brief pause.

"So, you're not going to tell me what you do with the peanut butter?"

"Not in this lifetime."

"Then I guess I'm going to end this conversation."

"Don't do that. There's got to be at least two or three Federal Communications Commission regulations we haven't violated yet."

"Sorry."

"You give up so-o-o-o-o easily."

"Are you free Saturday night?"

"Available, yes. Free, no."

"I'll call you later."

"I'll sit by the phone."

"Just one more thing."

"Sigh. That's what they all say."

"Any special brand of peanut butter?"

"The high price spread, of course."

"Goodbye, Hayley," Nick said, laughing.

"Goodbye...Michael," Hayley returned. A moment later, she dropped the telephone back into its cradle.

"Ahem."

She started slightly at the gruff sound, then slanted an inquiring glance at the doorway to her office.

"*Peanut butter?*" Al Kozlow queried, his eyebrows soaring toward his receding hairline.

"No, thank you," Hayley replied serenely.

Seven

The telephone rang a few minutes after noon on Saturday. Hayley was in the midst of cleaning her apartment.

Nick, she thought with a jittery sense of anticipation. She switched off her vacuum cleaner, crossed to the phone, and snatched up the receiver.

"Hello?" she asked a bit breathlessly.

"Hayley?"

"Oh... Mother." She swallowed a sigh of disappointment.

"Hello, dear. Have I gotten you at a bad time?"

"No, no. Not at all. I was just cleaning."

"You clean every Saturday, don't you?"

"That's right," Hayley concurred. She glanced around, absently noting that one of the two Oriental rugs on the living room floor was crooked.

"You're so organized," her mother observed. "Even as a little girl, you were organized. It was quite intimidating sometimes. Why, I'd be standing there, heading in a dozen different directions, completely lost, and you'd always know exactly where was where and what was what.''

Someone had to, Hayley reflected wryly. It was odd, though, now that she considered it. For a woman who could stand still, head in a dozen different directions, *and* be completely lost all at the same time, her mother had always seemed to end up precisely where she wanted to go.

She cocked her head, her gaze still on the out-of-alignment Oriental rug. It actually looked rather... interesting... set at that angle. And if she shifted the other rug a bit, it might create an attractive effect.

"How's everything with you, Mother?" she queried automatically.

"Lovely. Just lovely. I was calling to tell you that Elliot and I have finalized our travel plans."

"Terrific." She hoped that with Elliot involved in the proceedings, "finalized" would mean exactly that. Her mother generally defined the word as meaning slightly more definite than totally undecided.

"We're coming in with Muriel. My friend, Muriel Esterhaus? The one who does all the charity work? The gossip? You've never met her, but I must have mentioned her name."

"I'm pretty sure you have."

"Well, her husband has this marvelous corporate jet, so we're flying to New York with her. She's going to the fundraiser, too."

"That's nice." Hayley fluffed her hair, her attention wandering again.

Hmm, she mused. If she moved the rugs, she should probably shift the sofa, too. And the chairs that flanked it as well. And maybe she could get the chairs reupholstered while she was at it. Although the subtle, cream-on-cream fabric they were done in was perfectly fine, it suddenly struck her as being just a wee bit dull.

"Oh, it *is* nice, dear," her mother assured her. "Now, we'll be flying in late Tuesday night. I was hoping we could have dinner with you and Michael on Wednesday. He *is* going to be in town, isn't he?"

"Oh, yes," Hayley answered, fighting down a guilty laugh. "Operation: Mr. Wrong" would go forward. The only question was which Mr. Wrong was going to be the right one. She and Nick were supposed to get together this evening to decide that. "In, ah, some shape or form."

"I beg your pardon?"

"Nothing, Mother," Hayley said quickly, warning herself to watch it.

"You sound odd, Hayley. Are you all right?"

"Fine. Fine."

"There isn't a problem with Michael, is there?"

"No. Of course not. Not at all."

"Oh, good. I'm so eager to meet him. I've spent hours imagining what he's going to be like."

So have I, Hayley thought.

"Really?" she said aloud. "Well...he, ah, may surprise you."

"Do you think so? Hmm. You know, he reminded me of someone when I spoke with him on the phone. You'll never guess who."

Hayley tensed a little. "No, I probably won't," she agreed after a moment. "Who?"

"Your father."

"Ni—?" Hayley choked back the name. "Michael? *Michael* made you think of Daddy?"

"Mmm-hmm."

"That's...amazing, Mother."

"I don't know exactly what it was. But he definitely made me think of my dear Henry. In any case—does Wednesday night sound all right with you?"

"Yes. All right. Fine." *Nick O'Neill* had reminded her mother of her *father?* That was truly bizarre. From everything she knew, her father had been the model of rectitude and an emotional Rock of Gibraltar! Whereas Nick...

Whereas Nick might be trying to telephone her at this very moment. She really ought to get off the line.

"And what about the gala?"

"The gala?" Hayley echoed blankly.

"Would you and Michael like to come to the charity gala? It's been sold out for ages, of course. But Elliot can make arrangements to get you in. Elliot can make arrangements for anyone to do anything. He's so clever."

Hayley cleared her throat. "I'll have to speak to Michael."

"I hope he doesn't have to go out of town on business."

"Well—uh—" Hayley had to clear her throat again. "I, uh, never quite know what to expect with him."

"Are you *sure* you're all right, dear?"

"Yes. Positive." And she was going to be even *more* all right after "Operation: Mr. Wrong" was over and Michael Becker was finally out of her life forever.

Not that she wasn't going to miss Michael...after a fashion.

"You don't sound like yourself," Pamela Delaney Jerome Martinez de la Madrid Touissante Pynchley-Smythe Horowitz soon-to-be Parker declared worriedly from the other end of the line.

"I'm fine," her daughter returned firmly. "Really." And now she definitely had to hang up so Nick could call her.

"Well, if you're certain."

"I am. So. Just to confirm. You and Elliot are flying in a week from Tuesday, and Michael and I are having dinner with you the next night."

"Exactly. Oh, Hayley, I'm looking forward to this so much!"

"So am I, Mother. So am I."

After an affectionate exchange of farewells, both women disconnected. The phone rang the instant Hayley put it down. She picked it up once again.

"Hello?"

"Hayley."

"Nick!" She laughed a little, a sense of pleasure bubbling from deep inside her like a secret spring. "I was just talking about you."

"Oh?"

"Well, not about *you*," she amended, wondering about the edge in his voice. "About Michael."

"Oh." The edge was gone. The syllable was flat.

"My mother called."

"I see."

"She wanted to tell me—"

Bzzzzzz.

It was the security intercom.

"Hayley?"

"Would you hold on a second, please, Nick? Someone's buzzing me."

"No problem."

Hayley set down the phone and moved to the intercom panel. She pressed the Talk button.

"Yes?"

"Hiya. This is Franklin from Fantastic Florals. I've got a delivery here for a Ms. Hayley Jerome from a Mr. Becker. Can you buzz me in?"

Hayley was taken aback by this announcement. "Oh," she said after a moment. "Oh, of course." Thumbing the Enter button, she glanced over her shoulder at the phone. Flowers from *Nick?*

No, she corrected herself quickly. Flowers from Michael Becker.

There was a knock on her door less than thirty seconds later. Peering out through the peephole, Hayley saw a young man carrying a white oblong box and a large clipboard.

She undid the various and sundry locks on her door and opened it.

"You Ms. Jerome?"

"Yes."

"Great." The young man handed her the oblong box, then pulled a pen out of his pocket. He extended the pen and the clipboard. "Sign on the line with the X, willya, please?" he requested.

Hayley did as she was bidden. "Thank you," she said.

The young man shrugged. "Hey, I don't send the flowers. I just bring 'em. Have a nice day."

"You, too."

After shutting and locking the door once again, Hayley returned to the phone. She juggled the receiver and the box, finally wedging the former between her left ear and shoulder so she could open the letter.

"Hello?" Nick questioned.

"Yes," she said into the mouthpiece, slitting the tape that held the florist's package closed with her thumbnail. Her fingers were trembling slightly. "I'm here. I'm trying to—"

Hayley broke off on a gasp of pleasure as she lifted the top of the box off. There, nestled amid snowy-white tissue paper and a lining of feathery green ferns were twelve long-stemmed red roses.

"Hayley?"

"Oh, Nick," she breathed. "These flowers—oh. They're absolutely *beautiful*. But you really shouldn't have."

She heard a velvety chuckle from the other end of the line. The sound of it made her tingle. "I didn't," Nick said.

"But—"

"Michael did."

"Oh. Oh . . . yes."

"I—he—wasn't sure what kind of flowers you liked."

Hayley dipped her head and inhaled the heady fragrance from the boldly colored blossoms. "Well, one of you made a terrific guess," she declared after a moment.

"Are you . . . available . . . for tonight?" The pauses bracketing the adjective were barely perceptible yet unmistakably provocative.

Hayley cleared her throat, her imagination already starting to work. "Why, yes . . . Michael."

"Dinner? Dancing?"

"That sounds lovely."

"Have you ever been to—" He mentioned a very exclusive, very expensive supper club.

Hayley subdued a laugh. "I'm afraid that's not exactly my style," she said, her voice a bit huskier than normal.

"This evening it will be." The words were fraught with unspoken promises.

"I—" she touched the tip of her tongue to her upper lip "—see."

"I'll send a car for you at eight."

"A car?"

PEEK-A-BOO!

Free Gifts For You!

Look inside—Right Now!
We've got something
special just for you!

GIFTS

*There's no cost—
and no obligation
to buy anything!*

We'd like to send you free gifts to
introduce you to the benefits of the
Silhouette Reader Service™: free
home delivery of brand-new
Silhouette Desire® novels months
before they're available in stores,
and at a savings from the cover
price!

Accepting our free gifts places you
under no obligation to buy
anything ever. You may cancel the
Reader Service at any time, even
just after receiving your free gifts,
simply by writing "cancel" on
your statement or returning a
shipment of books to us at our
cost. But if you choose not to
cancel, every month we'll send
you six more Silhouette Desire®
novels and bill you just $2.47*
apiece—and there's **no** extra
charge for shipping and handling.
There are **no** hidden extras!

*Terms and prices subject to change without
notice. Sales tax applicable in N.Y. Offer limited
to one per household and not valid to current
Silhouette Desire® subscribers.

"At eight."

And then Nick—or was it Michael?—hung up.

Hayley placed her phone back into its cradle very slowly. Her heart, by contrast, was beating very quickly.

A dozen roses.

Dinner.

Dancing.

A car at eight...

Hayley glanced at the vacuum cleaner she'd abandoned when her mother had rung. After only a moment of internal debate, she succumbed to the clamor of her instincts and decided to forget the remainder of her regular Saturday routine.

Going shopping for something to wear that evening was much more important than sweeping floors or scrubbing tiles!

For a few sizzling moments, Nick forgot how to breathe.

"Surprised" was far too bland a word to describe what he felt as he watched Hayley Jerome move toward his table with a graceful, hip-swaying walk. "Stunned" was closer to the mark, but even that didn't capture the depth of his reaction.

Not even in his dreams...

Her fair hair was done up in a sensual riot of curls, swirls, and tendrils. The artlessly elegant style hinted that she'd either just tumbled out of a bed or was prepared to tumble into one in the very near future. It was the kind of coiffure that made a man's fingers itch to touch and tousle.

Her face was porcelain-pale and powdered, dominated by shimmering, shadowed eyes and an exquisitely defined, deeply rouged mouth. The eyes made promises. The mouth simply provoked.

And then there was Hayley's dress. It was a short, unadorned sluice of scarlet. The neckline was high, the sleeves were long, and the fabric caressed the lines of her body rather than clutching at them. Yet for all the apparent modesty of its styling, the overall effect of the garment was anything but demure.

Nick got to his feet, his heart thudding and his pulse thrumming.

For an instant Hayley thought her legs might simply give way beneath her.

The car Nick—or, rather, "Michael Becker"—had sent for her had been a black limousine complete with uniformed chauffeur, smoke-tinted windows, a telephone, television, and built-in bar. She'd found another florist's box sitting on the leather-covered back seat once the driver had handed her inside and closed the door. It, too, had contained a dozen crimson roses. The fragrance of the flowers had blended with the subtly expensive smell of the car's plush interior.

She'd been welcomed to the supper club as though she was a long-standing and much valued customer. A murmured mention of the name "Michael Becker" had increased the obsequiousness of the maître d'hôtel's eager-to-be-of-service smile.

"But, of course, *madame,*" the dapperly dressed man had responded in an unctuous voice. "*Monsieur* Becker is expecting you. If you will permit me to escort you to his table? This way, *s'il vous plaît.*"

Hayley had followed the maître d'hôtel, pleasantly conscious of the fact that she was drawing openly interested glances from a number of the club's other patrons. Under different circumstances, the attention probably would have embarrassed her. But, in this instance, she relished it.

And then she saw him.

Nick.

Michael Becker.

Her awareness of her surroundings—of other people—narrowed in the space of a single heartbeat. A feverish thrill ran through her. She felt herself flush.

Dressed in the black and white severity of a tuxedo, Nick radiated a darkly virile, dangerously potent aura that lured her from halfway across the room. His thick hair was combed back from his brow, emphasizing the lean angularity of his face. His expression was austere until their gazes met.

And then he smiled at her, his even teeth showing white, his dimple flashing roguishly to the left of his mouth. That's when the bones in Hayley's legs seemed to turn to water.

Somehow she made it to Nick's table. He was standing up by this time, utterly at ease yet undeniably on alert. He looked suave, sophisticated, and just slightly unsavory. He was the sexy as hell embodiment of every worried mother's nightmares and every wayward daughter's dreams.

"Madame—" the maître d' gestured *"—monsieur."*

Mesmerized, Hayley extended her right hand to Nick. He grasped it and raised it to his lips. The brief press of his mouth against her knuckles sent a white-hot quiver of response arrowing up her arm. She felt her nipples tighten beneath the bodice of her dress.

"I'm pleased you could join me," he told her, his voice low and liquid.

"I'm pleased you invited me," she returned, sinking into the seat opposite him.

The table was set for two, with crisp linen, polished silver, and sparkling crystal. There was a silver ice bucket with a foil-topped bottle protruding from it sitting to Nick's right. The maître d' indicated it with a nod of his head.

"Monsieur?" he inquired.

"Yes, please," Nick responded, never taking his eyes off Hayley.

Neither of them spoke for several moments. Hayley shifted a little in her seat, conscious of the sleek friction of the fabric of her dress against her body. She crossed her legs, pressing her thighs together. A ripple of pleasure radiated upward from her core.

"I took the liberty of ordering champagne," Nick eventually commented, watching Hayley's crystalline blue eyes darken and her lids flutter down for just an instant. He saw her lips part and caught a brief glimpse of pink tongue. He recalled the flavor of those sensuously shaped lips and the texture of that sinuous tongue in arousing, erotic detail. "I hope it's to your taste."

"I'm sure it will be," she assured him, nodding her head. The bold, red-jeweled earrings she was wearing danced against her cheeks.

The maître d' had popped the cork on the champagne bottle by this time. He deftly poured a glass of the golden, bubbling liquid for Hayley, then one for Nick. After politely ascertaining that he could be of no further service, he placed the bottle back in the ice bucket and moved away.

Keeping her gaze fixed unwaveringly on Nick's face, Hayley slowly curled her fingers around the fragile stem of her champagne flute. She lifted the glass. Her ripe mouth curved into a smile that made Nick profoundly grateful he had a strong heart. Her expression packed enough voltage to send a man with cardiac problems into arrest.

"To taking liberties," she murmured throatily.

Nick lifted his own glass and clinked it gently against hers. "To surprises," he returned.

They dined and flirted, flirted and dined. Except for the delicious tidbits Nick fed her from his own plate, Hayley never remembered much about what she'd eaten. She couldn't even recall whether she'd been hungry.

After the meal, Nick asked her to dance. She accepted eagerly.

Despite the decidedly French flavor of the supper club's cuisine, its small band favored a distinctly Latin beat. The music it played was spicily syncopated and insinuatingly sexual.

Nick danced as he seemed to do so many other things— superbly. He partnered Hayley with effortless expertise through variations on the merengue, the salsa, and the samba. There was never a hint of awkwardness. Never a moment's hesitation.

Hayley felt as though she and Nick had been dancing together for years. It wasn't a matter of his leading or her following. It was a physical harmony she'd never experienced before. And the intuitive attunement seemed to intensify with each passing measure of music. Hayley let herself surrender to the exhilaration of it.

The music communicated an enticingly elemental message. Thighs brushed. Hips shifted. Hands lingered a second or two longer than necessary. Hayley's gaze caught Nick's and clung. She couldn't have looked away from him if she'd wanted to. A rush of warmth suffused her body.

The fabric of her dress rippled over her skin. The flashy drops dangling from her earlobes bounced and swung. Hayley felt Nick's palms curve to fit her waist then slide backward until his fingertips met in the hollow at the base of her spine.

And then the music altered. The key changed. The rhythm turned languid and alluring. Nick pulled Hayley close, fitting her against him. Soft to hard. Heat to hunger.

He sensed a split second of resistance, then felt her melt. He held her even closer.

The yielding sway of her body. The elusively sweet scent of her skin. The winsome sound of her sigh. These things exploded in Nick's senses, leaving him shaken to the core. Desire prowled through him like a jungle cat, raking him with fiery claws.

He knew there was no way to disguise the strength of his physical reaction. The already-taut muscles of his belly clenched. The masculine flesh lower down grew heavy and hard.

He wanted. Dear God, how he wanted. And for how long! It seemed like a lifetime.

Dipping his head, Nick brushed his mouth briefly against the side of Hayley's slender throat. He felt the leap of her pulse with his lips, felt the quiver that ran through her with his entire body. Her hands moved restlessly, sliding up his arms then moving inward to press flat against his chest. The heat from her palms and widespread fingers seemed to burn straight through the fabric of his evening jacket and dress shirt.

He let his own hands travel upward, relishing the moment when the smooth material of Hayley's dress gave way to the even silkier texture of her skin. The garment that was so modestly styled in the front plunged to a deep V in the back, baring a creamy expanse of feminine flesh. Nick stroked the balls of his thumbs along the supple line of her spine, his self-control fraying in the face of irresistible speculation about whether she was wearing anything beneath her dress besides stockings and perfume. Hayley arched in answer to his caress, her fingers clutching at him.

Finally the song came to a close. The final notes seemed to hang in the air, reverberating, then reluctantly faded away. The other dancers on the floor broke apart and began applauding. After a few seconds Hayley and Nick did the same.

Hayley's blood was simmering in her veins. She felt as though she'd been encased in a shimmering envelope where every physical sensation was multiplied a hundredfold. She gazed up at Nick, remembering the two kisses they'd shared. She was suddenly hungry to sample the tastes and textures of his mouth again. To experience the satiny firmness of his lips and the rough velvet glide of his tongue for a third... fourth... and fifth time.

She was trembling, and she knew it was because of him.

Hayley whispered Nick's name.

He said hers in return, his voice husky, his smoke-and-emerald eyes caressing her face. Then, slipping an arm around her waist, he guided her back to their table.

Nick was in the process of reseating her when Hayley heard him suck in his breath like a man who'd just taken a blow to the stomach. She sensed, rather than saw, him stiffen. Shifting in her chair, she looked up at him. What she saw in his face chilled her to the marrow.

"Nick?" she asked uncertainly. His angular features had hardened into an unreadable mask, totally devoid of emotion. "What—"

She broke off, flinching slightly as his fingers bit warningly into her shoulders. Nick bent forward to murmur in her ear.

"You remember the snake I told you about last Saturday?" he asked urgently. "The one who slithered away?"

Dazed as she was by Nick's frightening transformation, Hayley needed a moment to place the reference. Once she did she gasped, her eyes widening in appalled understanding. Dear God, was he telling her—?

"Yeah," Nick said, grimly confirming the conclusion she'd drawn. "He just slithered in, and he's heading this way. You're going to have to follow my lead, angel. This is a con for keeps. The main thing you have to remember is that my name is Neil James and that I'm paying you for your company."

There *was* something reptilian about the silver-haired man who approached their table a few moments later. At first Hayley thought the impression was created by the gliding smoothness of his gait. Then she realized it had much more to do with his eyes. They were a peculiar shade of gray. Flat. Frigid. Like disks of chilled lead. It took all her self-discipline not to shudder the first time she felt his gaze move over her.

"*Monsieur* James," the man said to Nick, an odd smile ghosting around the corners of his thin-lipped mouth. He was impeccably dressed in an immaculately cut dinner jacket. Hayley estimated he was in his early fifties.

"Mr. de Sante," Nick returned, still standing next to Hayley's chair.

"It's been—what?" The older man gestured with his left hand. A wafer-thin gold wristwatch glinted beneath the cuff of his shirt.

"A few years."

"They appear to have been felicitous ones for you, *mon ami*." The accent that colored de Sante's excellent English was an amalgam of French and something else Hayley couldn't identify.

"No more than for you, Philippe."

De Sante's lips drew back from his teeth for a moment. His smile was like a paper cut—razor thin and capable of drawing blood. "I have been fortunate," he admitted. His tone—to say nothing of his obviously custom-tailored clothing—suggested he was understating the case by a significant degree. "I have also thought about you more than a few times since our last meeting."

"Oh?"

"Mmm. Considering how skillfully you evaded the disaster that overtook our mutual acquaintances, I could not help but speculate that perhaps you might have played a role in precipitating their downfall."

Somehow Hayley managed not to stiffen at this barbed remark.

"Really?" Nick sounded amused by the not-so-veiled accusation of treachery. "What a coincidence. I couldn't help speculating exactly the same thing about you for exactly the same reason."

There was a tense moment, then the other man chuckled. *"Touché,"* he acknowledged. "Your wit is as quick as I remember it." He paused a beat, then shifted his gaze to Hayley, surveying her with unnerving thoroughness. "Your taste in women, however, has infinitely improved. This is—?"

Afterward Hayley tried to figure out what possessed her to do what she did next. She never succeeded in coming up with a rational explanation.

Without waiting for Nick to speak, she extended her right hand to Philippe de Sante. Meeting his assessing stare with just a hint of challenge, she favored him with what she hoped was the smile of a woman who understood her desirability and had long since put a very high price on it.

"I'm Michelle Becker," she said simply.

Eight

She was almost incandescent with excitement, flying on the adrenaline the stress of the past few hours had pumped into her system. Having had that stress lifted hadn't brought her down an inch, either. If anything, the sudden relief had probably heightened her sense of euphoria.

Nick watched Hayley flitting around her living room like a butterfly. He understood exactly what she was experiencing. He understood it because he'd been there himself.

Unfortunately understanding her feelings did nothing to help him control his own. Euphoria was not his problem at the moment. His problem was that there was an emotional war raging within him and he had no way to call a truce.

Half of him wanted to grab Hayley and shake her until her teeth rattled. The other half wanted to sweep her up into his arms and kiss her senseless. Both halves wanted to read her the riot act.

Did she have any idea what kind of risk she'd run at the supper club? Nick wondered furiously, jerking loose his black bow tie. Never mind that her improvised identity had meshed seamlessly with his previously established cover. Never mind that she'd kept her cool better than some of the so-called professionals he'd worked with. Never mind that Philippe de Sante had bought her performance as an ultra-expensive call girl hook, line, and sinker. When he thought about the chances she'd taken tonight he wanted to...to...

Dammit, he didn't know what he wanted to do! Maybe he'd shake Hayley until her teeth rattled and *then* kiss her senseless. Or maybe vice versa. Hell, maybe he'd do both at the same time!

Meanwhile, he had to make it absolutely and utterly clear to his erstwhile lady of the evening that the time for fun and games was over. Finished. Done with. He'd made up his mind about that. There weren't going to be any more Michael Beckers. And no more Michelle Beckers, either. There weren't going to be any more *anybodies* except the two of them—Nick and Hayley, Hayley and Nick.

"We did it, Nick," Hayley exulted giddily, kicking off her high-heeled evening sandals. She'd already shed her coat and tossed aside the small beaded purse she'd been carrying. "He believed every word. De Sante believed *every single word*. Every syllable!"

"Hayley—" Nick began determinedly, moving toward her.

"I never knew it was like this," she chattered on. "This is why you love undercover work, isn't it, Nick? I mean—the rush! Pretending. Pitting yourself against someone else. Putting it all on the line. And when it works! Oh, God, *when it works!* To have the sense that you've got someone hooked. Really hooked. Only you can't be absolutely sure, can you? There's always that edge of doubt. That fear that maybe *you're* the one being conned, not the one doing the conning. But that's part of the attraction isn't—"

"*Hayley.*" Nick caught her by the shoulders, holding hard enough to get her attention but not enough to hurt. "*Stop it.*"

She did. The touch of his hands, the tone of his voice, shut Hayley up for a good ten seconds. During those ten silent seconds Nick had more than enough time to question the wisdom of getting near enough to smell the sweetly sensual fragrance of her skin and feel the alluring warmth of her body.

He would swear later that Hayley took the initiative, but he was never entirely sure. It really made no difference which one of them closed the space between them. All that mattered was that one moment they were separated by inches and the next they were locked in an embrace.

His mouth met hers, mating with it in a sizzling certainty that this was something that was meant to be. Hayley's lips opened beneath his, and he took what was offered with a searching sweep of his tongue. The heady flavor of her sluiced through him, whetting his appetite for more. He feasted on the yielding softness of her mouth, claiming its secrets with deep, delving strokes.

Hayley went up on her stockinged toes, pressing against him, instinctively seeking the most intimate fit possible. Nick's hands slid downward from her shoulders, stroking the bared skin of her back as though he could absorb the taste of it through his palms. He tasted the taut slenderness of her waist, then cupped the gentle swell of her derriere through the sleek fabric of her dress. Her body tightened in answer to his caress.

Nick lifted his mouth from hers for an instant, then caught her lower lip between his teeth. He bit down with exquisite care and felt Hayley quiver. He licked the tiny mark he'd left on her petal pink flesh and heard her give a soft purr of pleasure. Her breath misted over his skin for a split second, and then she began kissing him in the same hungry way he'd been kissing her.

Where his hands had moved down, Hayley's glided in the opposite direction, smoothing up his jacketed chest and easing over his broad shoulders to lock behind his neck. Her tongue teased and tantalized. She exhaled on a sigh when he responded in kind. His tongue thrust smoothly between her parted lips and teeth, evoking thoughts of an even more intimate joining. Her fingers spasmed, her nails biting briefly into his flesh.

It was that fleeting sting of pain that caused Nick to lift his mouth from Hayley's for a second time. He knew he wanted more—much more—than kisses and caresses. He wanted to make love with Hayley. He wanted to feel her move beneath him. To hear her breathless cries of rapture. To know what it was like to be gloved within the honeyed heat of her body. But he had to be sure, absolutely sure, that that was what she wanted, too. He had to be sure that Hayley knew exactly what she was doing and with whom she was doing it.

The sight of her kiss-rouged lips shook his resolve. The yearning look in her brilliant blue eyes nearly shattered it.

"Nick?" Her fingers caught at the thick, dark hair at the back of his head.

"Tell me what you want, angel," he said, his voice roughened by the force of his restraint.

She blinked, her breath coming out in shaky little snatches. "You," she whispered with devastating simplicity. "I want you, Nick."

"Me?" he echoed tautly. "Not Michael Becker? Not some...fantasy?"

The smile Hayley had given Philippe de Sante had been calculated in the extreme. The one that curved her mouth now was utterly without artifice. It seared through Nick like a bolt of lightning, electrifying every cell of his brain and body.

"You," she repeated huskily. "Nicholas...James... O'Neill."

Nick reclaimed Hayley's lips almost before she finished speaking. A moment later he swept her up into his arms and carried her into her bedroom.

Although he'd seen the plastic packet of birth control pills in Hayley's medicine cabinet two weeks before when he'd gone looking for aspirin, Nick had to ask.

"Are you protected?" he questioned, shedding his tuxedo jacket and casting it aside. He'd already rid himself of his shoes.

Hayley, who was standing only a few feet away, nodded once.

"Do you want me to use—?"

She shook her head, her earrings swaying with the movement.

"You're sure?"

"Yes," she affirmed.

He opened his arms. She went to him, stepping into his embrace, turning her face up to receive his kiss. She parted her lips, hungry for the taste and heat of his mouth and tongue. Nick teased her—and himself—for a few seconds, then gave what was wanted so plainly and took what was offered so freely. Hayley melted against him with a throaty moan of satisfaction.

She trembled as Nick caressed her from shoulder to breast, from breast to hip, then lower still. His hands stroked over the fragile fabric of her dress, working an incendiary magic on her body. She closed her eyes, twisting in response to his touch. A shimmering heat suffused her, making her shudder like the victim of a raging fever.

Blindly, Hayley began to undo the front of his dress shirt. It was no simple task—passion and impatience made her fingers less than steady. But she finally finished what she'd started. She yanked the garment free of the waistband of his trousers, then pressed her hands against him. With savoring slowness, she began to explore the dark, dense hair that whorled across his chest and the taut bands of muscle beneath.

Nick stiffened as Hayley's questing fingers found his nipples. His breath jammed at the top of his throat as she scraped the edges of her nails over the aching nubs of flesh. The delicately deliberate torture was almost more than he could take. He groaned.

Hayley smiled when she heard the sound, a wild sense of womanly power burning through her. She dipped her head, touching her mouth to his naked flesh. The springy texture of his chest hair teased her lips. The salty tang of his skin tantalized her tongue.

"Hayley—angel—" Nick gasped, jolted by the feel of her mouth. After several endlessly erotic moments, he threaded his fingers into the silken tumble of her fair hair and brought her head up. An instant later, he captured her lips with his own.

Hayley surrendered to the devouring kiss. She arched against Nick, angling her face, offering her mouth for an even deeper possession. While one of Nick's hands stayed tangled in her hair, the other flowed down her back in a fluid, passionate sweep.

His shirt went first, then her dress. His earlier suppositions about what she was—and wasn't—wearing beneath the garment proved to be arousingly accurate.

"You are . . . so beautiful . . ." Nick told Hayley hoarsely. Except for her sheer nylon stockings and a few lacy scraps of scarlet satin, she was naked. He cupped her bared breasts, his thumbs brushing across their rosy tips. Her nipples stiffened and she gave a soft, broken cry.

"N-Nick . . . oh, Nick . . ."

More kisses. More caresses. Finally Nick scooped Hayley up and carried her the few steps to her bed. He lay her down on the mattress, stroking her with his eyes and his hands, murmuring words meant to pleasure and praise. Finally he straightened and took a step back. Swiftly, he shucked off the remainder of his clothes.

Hayley caught her breath at her first glimpse of Nick's full nakedness. A thrill ran through her, making her body tingle with anticipation. She experienced a very feminine pang of fear, too. Not that she was afraid Nick would hurt her. She would never think him capable of that. But his size—and the potency of his arousal—made her feel fragile.

As he had so many times before, Nick seemed to sense the essence of her thoughts. "We're made for each other, Hayley," he told her huskily, moving back to the bed. "Don't worry. I know my own strength."

And then he stretched out beside her and began to show her the truth of his words.

There was nowhere Nick didn't touch, didn't test. His hands molded her, massaged her, made her tremble and gasp. His fingers feathered up the soft skin of her inner thighs then brushed through the pale cluster of curls that sheltered her womanly secrets. He parted the slick, petaled flesh and fondled her with exquisite restraint. He felt her body tighten for an instant, then melt like sun-warmed honey.

Hayley moaned his name. Aroused and emboldened, she began to explore Nick as intimately as he was exploring her. She relished each and every detail, reveled in each and every discovery. There were moments when she was tempted to linger over a new taste or texture, but there was always something even more tantalizing to claim her attention.

Time stretched. Slowed. Eventually seemed to stop flowing entirely. For Hayley there was nothing but heat and hunger and the man who was the source of both. When she felt the first nudge of his knee between her thighs, she opened to him without hesitation.

Hayley cried out in wonderment when Nick joined them with a single, sliding stroke.

The sensation of sheathing himself deep inside Hayley's body nearly undid Nick. His control had begun unraveling the moment he'd kissed her in the living room and it was fraying thread by thread. He forced himself to go very still, ruthlessly holding himself balanced on the brink of a release so intensely desired it was almost agonizing.

"Nick...oh, please...Nick..." Hayley pleaded raggedly, running her hands urgently up and down his sweat-sheened back.

Finally, when he could endure it no longer, Nick began to move within her. Slowly. Deeply. After the first few thrusts Hayley's hips lifted in a counterpointed response. Her body accepted his possession without inhibition, wordlessly urging him on...and on. He groaned as her satin flesh closed around him, caressing him with a sensual completeness that he'd never believed existed outside of dreams.

The tempo of their passion accelerated. Faster. Then faster still. They burned with the same fever, they sought the same cure.

"Hayley... Hayley..."

"Nick... yes..."

Yes.

And yes again.

Yes!

Ecstasy was a flame. It burned brightly, boldly, and beyond human control. Hayley and Nick clung to each other and let themselves be consumed by the white-hot bliss of it.

Afterward, spent and finally satisfied, they slept.

The soft puff of Hayley's breath and the dreamy drift of her fingers woke Nick early the next morning. His fair-haired lover of one night was snuggling against him, pleasuring him even in sleep. She murmured something that might have been his name as he gently but firmly trapped her wandering hands, then shifted in a way that made his muscles clench and his pulse kick.

He wanted her again. Never mind the three times they'd already made love. He wanted her again and he wanted her now.

There was nothing to stop him from rousing Hayley with kisses and caresses. Nothing to stop him from easing himself into the sweet heat of her feminine core as he ached to do. Nothing except his awareness that when he thought of "wanting" Hayley Jerome, the wanting went far beyond sexual desire.

He was in love with her. Irrevocably, irreversibly in love with her.

But how did Hayley feel about him? That was something Nick still didn't know. He wasn't at all certain she knew herself. That she wanted him was obvious. But whether her definition of "wanting" was as all-encompassing as his, he couldn't say.

Hayley shifted again, curling into him like a kitten seeking warmth. She exhaled on a languid sigh. The pouting tips of her naked breasts brushed against his chest, triggering a surge of response between his thighs.

Nick realized he had to get up. Immediately. Not in a couple of minutes. Not in a couple of seconds. He had to get up *right now*. What had happened the night before had happened and he was profoundly grateful for it, but he couldn't allow it to happen again until he and Hayley had talked.

Carefully, Nick extricated himself from the seductive tangle of limbs and bed linen. Then he eased himself off the bed and stood up. At the same time, Hayley rolled over onto her stomach and burrowed her face into the pillow where his head had lain only a few moments before.

Nick gazed down at Hayley, his memory jumping back to the night he'd undressed her and discovered that the Ice Princess wore red-hot satin underwear.

Had that been the instant he'd tumbled into love? he wondered.

Maybe.

Or had it happened before that? he asked himself. Had it happened while he'd been listening to Hayley unfold her lunatic scheme involving Michael Becker?

Again, maybe.

Of course, the seeds of the emotions now blossoming in his heart and soul might very well have been planted in the first moment he'd laid eyes on her. For all its brevity, theirs had been no ordinary introduction.

"Mmm." Hayley changed position again, clutching at the sheets.

Breakfast, Nick decided swiftly, swallowing hard. I'll go make her some breakfast.

On his way to the kitchen, he detoured to the bathroom and took a shower.

A very quick but very cold one.

Something wasn't right.

The realization insinuated itself into Hayley's sleep-hazed brain like a half-stifled whisper. Not quite loud enough to be understood, yet too audible to be ignored.

"Ummm...nnnnn..." she mumbled, wrinkling her nose and squirming around.

Something was...missing.

"Ni...mmmmm...ick," she mumbled again.

Not something.

Someone.

Nick.

Hayley's whole body jerked. Her eyelids popped open. She lurched up into a sitting position and remained there, trembling, while her brain replayed the events of the night before.

"Oh, God," she whispered, crossing her arms in front of her breasts. She glanced around the room, silently cataloging the various articles of clothing strewn on the floor. "What have I done?"

Done? her mind echoed. What had she *done?* She'd done what she'd wanted to do almost from the first second she'd met Nick O'Neill.

She'd made love with him. Wildly. Wantonly. Without a shred of inhibition. Again and again, she'd made love with him. And even now, there was a throb of yearning deep inside that urged her to—

A sudden clatter of metal followed by a muffled curse made Hayley stiffen. *What in the world?*

And then she knew.

It was Nick. In the kitchen.

Making a mess.

Creating chaos.

Changing everything around to suit his own consistently inconsistent whims.

Nicholas James O'Neill, imposing *his* unruly imprint on *her* carefully ordered, meticulously organized kitchen.

But Hayley didn't mind. She didn't mind the idea of the mess or the chaos or the changes. She didn't mind, and the realization of why she didn't shook her right down to what she'd believed were the rock-steady foundations of her life.

She didn't mind...*because she'd fallen in love with him.*

"Oh, God," Hayley breathed, grappling with a truth that threatened to upset her entire world. "What have I done?"

*   *   *

The first word that popped into Nick's head when he saw
Hayley standing in the doorway of her kitchen had four letters. None of them was *L, O, V,* or *E.*

He'd thought he'd prepared himself for every possible
morning-after-the-night-before scenario. Unfortunately he'd
thought wrong. He'd never bothered to prepare himself for
the possibility that the woman he wanted to spend the rest
of his life with would once more confront him with anxi-
ety-clouded eyes and a guarded manner.

Dammit! he swore silently. Not again!

It was back. That inexplicable quality of fear he'd felt
radiating from Hayley the first time they'd met was back,
and he still didn't understand its source.

She looked so damned vulnerable it hurt. Her hair was
tousled like a little girl's. Her face was scrubbed clean, innocent of all cosmetic artifice. Her body was pristinely co-
cooned in the same loose-fitting white terry cloth robe she'd
worn the last time he'd been in her apartment.

His impulse was to take the four strides needed to oblit-
erate the physical distance between them and enfold Hayley
into an embrace. But his instincts warned him not to do
anything so overt. His instincts also told him to swallow the
declarations he'd intended to make.

"Good morning," Hayley said finally, forcing herself to
meet Nick's gaze. Her palms were wet, her throat was dry
and her heart was pounding like a tom-tom. She'd never
wanted any part of love and this was why. It was an emotion she couldn't control, a variable that inevitably upset
even the most carefully calculated equation. And when love
involved a man like Nick O'Neill—!

"Good morning," he answered, setting down the con-
tainer of orange juice he was holding. "Did you sleep well?"

His question indicated nothing but polite concern.
Nonetheless, Hayley felt herself flush as the inquiry un-
leashed the flood of memories she'd been trying to hold at
bay. Something contracted deep in her belly.

"Yes," she said after a long moment, desperately wishing Nick had put on more than the trousers of his tuxedo

when he'd gotten out of bed. Her gaze was irresistibly drawn down his torso to the fine, dark line of hair that arrowed beneath his snug-fitting waistband. She dragged her eyes back up to his face once again, her cheeks burning. "And...you?"

"Fine," he replied, schooling his expression into neutrality. What in the world was wrong? Was it something he'd done? Hadn't done? Said? Hadn't said? He'd expected there might be a little awkwardness, a little uncertainty, between them this morning. But nothing like this!

Was it possible that the night before hadn't been as good for her as it had been for him? Was it possible that she hadn't felt what he'd felt, sensed what he'd sensed? Their lovemaking had seemed so right to him. So absolutely, utterly right...

"I, ah, heard you out here when I woke up," Hayley remarked, twisting the belt of her robe.

"Really?" It was an inane thing to say and Nick knew it but somehow inanities struck him as his safest option at the moment. He gestured smoothly. "I thought I'd make you some breakfast."

Hayley managed a little smile. "I see."

Half of her envied Nick's air of ease. The other half resented the hell out of it. How could he be so casual? She didn't expect—didn't want!—undying protestations of love from him. But she ached for some small sign that what had happened the night before had mattered to him.

Silence stretched between them like a nylon thread, growing more and more taut with each passing second. Nick was the one who finally snapped it.

"I've lost your respect, haven't I?" he said, deciding to risk an appeal to Hayley's quirky sense of humor. Laughter had helped ease other difficult moments between them. With luck, it might do the same now. It certainly couldn't make things much worse.

"Wh-what?" Hayley stammered, bewildered.

Nick manufactured a sigh. "I let you have your way with me, and now you don't respect me anymore."

Hayley stared at him for several seconds. A joke? Nick was making a *joke* at a time like this? How could he possibly be so totally insensitive, so monumentally—

She never finished the thought. Instead, she caught a gleam in his changeable eyes and suddenly realized what he was attempting to do. Outrage gave way to understanding gave way to reluctant amusement in quick succession.

There were very few people who'd have the nerve to take a humorous tack in a situation like this, Hayley reflected wryly. Even fewer who'd be capable of making it work. Nick O'Neill was plainly one of that elite number.

The odd thing was, she had the distinct feeling she could be one of them, too...if she chose.

"Hayley?" Nick asked cautiously, trying to gauge her expression.

Hayley cocked her head and narrowed her eyes. "Tell me, Nick," she invited dulcetly. "Just what makes you think I respected you *before* you let me have my way with you?"

Genuinely startled by this riposte, Nick sucked in his breath at the same time he started to laugh. He nearly choked. "Well," he finally managed to get out, "a man can always hope, can't he?"

"I suppose," she conceded with a delicate shrug.

There was a brief silence as Nick recovered his breath. Then he opened his arms.

After a fractional hesitation, Hayley moved to him. A quiver ran through her as his arms closed around her. The embrace was a gentle one. She closed her eyes as she felt him press his mouth against her hair.

"It feels good to hold you, Hayley," Nick told her softly.

"It feels good to be held," she murmured in return.

Nick allowed a few seconds tick by. Then he said carefully, "About last night—"

Hayley lifted her head to look at him, her eyes wide and wary.

"Look, it happened," he told her, the necessity of holding back the words he really wanted to say leaving an ashy taste in his mouth. "I wanted you. You wanted me. And it just happened. It doesn't have to—" he paused, searching for the right word "—to *change* anything between us."

Hayley didn't know whether the emotion surging through her was relief or regret or a mixture of both. "In other words," she began, "you think we can—"

She never got the chance to finish. Someone started knocking on the door to her apartment. This was no tentative rapping, either. A little bit harder and it would have been out-and-out pounding.

Hayley and Nick broke apart. She started automatically for the door. He caught the sleeve of her robe and pulled her up short.

"What—?"

"Don't people normally buzz you on the security intercom before they show up at your door?" he asked sharply.

"Well, yes, but—"

"'Yes, but,' nothing. I called an old buddy of mine before you woke up. The one who gave me the official unofficial ID. He was very interested to hear that Monsieur de Sante is slithering around Manhattan."

Hayley's heart skipped a beat. Her body tensed. "Are you saying—"

Knock! Knock! Knock!

"Miss Jerome?" a man's voice questioned from the other side of the door. "Miss Hayley Jerome?"

"Who is it?" Nick called back.

"O'Neill?" came the gravelly response. "Is that you, O'Neill?"

Hayley gasped in horror, recognizing her boss's voice.

"Easy, angel," Nick advised calmly, moving toward the door.

Knock! Knock! Knock!

"Open up!" the first voice ordered. "Official business. FBI."

"Ohmigod." Hayley groaned.

Nick undid the locks and opened the door, taking care to shield Hayley's body with his own as he did so. The grim expression on Al Kozlow's face told him most of the story.

The squared jaws and steely eyes of the blue-suited men flanking him filled in the blanks.

"Nicholas O'Neill?" one of the suits questioned.

"Yeah."

"Hayley Jerome?"

"Y-yes."

"I'm Special Agent Leahy. This is Special Agent Oliver. We want to ask you some questions about your association with Philippe de Sante."

Nine

"I never should have made you take a vacation," Al Kozlow declared disgustedly once Nick and Hayley had finished explaining how they'd come to be on such apparently chummy terms with a man who was under surveillance by the federal government.

"Excuse me?" questioned Agent Leahy. Like his partner, Oliver, he was a man with no distinguishing features. He was in his mid-thirties, with medium brown hair and medium brown eyes. His height and weight were utterly average. Nick had him pegged as a blend-in field operative with bureaucratic tendencies. He sensed that Oliver, for all his surface blandness, was made of tougher stuff. He also had the feeling Oliver worked hard at making himself easy to overlook. Leahy's lack of distinction appeared to have been bestowed on him at birth.

"Vacation," Kozlow repeated, studying his top undercover operative with dolefully accusing eyes. "I should have figured, O'Neill. I really should have figured. I know what you're like when you've got too much time and too little to fill it with. I should have figured you'd get up to something. And as for you, Jerome—" He shifted his gaze toward Hayley, shaking his head. "What can I say? I expect this kind of lunacy from O'Neill. But you? The Ice Princess paper shuffler? I'm not saying I haven't been waiting for you to break out and show me what you've really got. To tell you the truth, I have been. Which is why I didn't press last week when I walked in on you having an X-rated telephone conversation about peanut butter—"

"Peanut butter?" Leahy interrupted again, stiffening like a bird dog going on point.

Hayley flushed hotly and stole a sideward glance at Nick. She saw one corner of his mouth twist. Then, as though he sensed her scrutiny, he angled his head in her direction and gave her a quick wink.

While the wink did absolutely nothing to cool her cheeks, Hayley felt reassured by it. She knew that had been Nick's intention. Throughout this entire humiliating session he'd been there for her, rock solid and ready with an encouraging nod or a succinctly worded answer.

There had been no physical contact, however. None at all. He hadn't touched her once since their embrace in the kitchen had ended.

Kozlow nailed Special Agent Leahy with a disdainful look. "If you have to ask about peanut butter, you don't want to know," he stated, then transferred his attention back to Hayley. "I'm speechless, Jerome," he declared. "O'Neill conning you into something like this, I could believe. But *you* conning *him?*"

"She didn't con me, Al," Nick said sharply. "I volunteered."

"But the scam was her idea," Leahy clarified.

"That's right," Hayley affirmed in a steady voice. She'd already noticed that the four men sitting in her living room seemed determined to talk around her as much as possible. Nick, she sensed, was doing it out of a desire to shield her from the inherent unpleasantness of the current situation. She wasn't certain about the other men's motives. Maybe they had problems treating a woman who was wearing nothing but a bathrobe as an equal.

"And this Michael Becker doesn't exist except in her imagination," Leahy persisted, still addressing Nick.

"That's right," Hayley repeated with a slight edge, rubbing her palms against the nubby material of her robe.

"And mine," Nick added.

"And my mother's," Hayley tacked on.

"And her mother's fiancé's," Nick noted.

"Who just happens to be a former member of the U.S. House of Representatives who used to serve on one of the intelligence oversight committees," Oliver concluded sourly. "Wonderful."

"But you've been pretending to be this Michael Becker during the past two weeks as a—uh—favor to Miss Jerome," Leahy picked up, his voice carefully kept free of sexual innuendo. He'd made one mildly salacious comment near the start of the interview. Nick had responded with a quietly explicit statement about what he'd do if the agent made another such remark within Hayley's hearing. "Is that right, Mr. O'Neill?"

"The two weeks he was *supposed* to be on vacation," Al Kozlow grumbled.

"Yes, Agent Leahy," Nick answered. "That's right."

"And you were pretending to be this Michael Becker last night until de Sante showed up. At which point you started pretending to be Neil James and Miss Jerome started pretending to be—uh—uh—"

"*Michelle* Becker," Hayley and Nick supplied in unison, then traded looks.

"And de Sante bought it." This was from Oliver.

Nick studied the FBI man for several seconds. Finally, he thought. The tea party had just come to an end. It was time to get down to the nitty-gritty.

"You've got a roll of pictures taken of the three of us last night at the supper club," he pointed out after a moment, indicating the black-and-white photographs spread out on the coffee table in front of the sofa where he and Hayley were sitting. Out of the corner of his eye, he saw Hayley shift suddenly and wondered if she had an inkling that things were about to turn serious. Probably. As he'd told her in this very room fifteen days before, she had terrific instincts. He only wished he knew what those instincts were telling her about him. "What do you think?"

"I think it's really strange that your old buddy de Sante just happened to show up in the same place you and Miss Jerome were playing this little masquerade of yours."

"De Sante was never my buddy."

"You dealt with him four years ago."

"A sting."

"Which he walked away from."

"Because some desk jockey from D.C. who didn't know the difference between undercover work and underarm deodorant blew the gaff before the payoff."

"So you say, O'Neill."

"So I know, Oliver. I was there. We dropped twelve bad guys in that operation. We also recovered twenty million dollars worth of stolen military hardware you Feebies couldn't have found if you'd had printed instructions. If I could have nailed de Sante, I would have. But he was long gone before the bust went down and he didn't leave a trail. He never does. The son of a bitch is slick. No evidence. No indictments. No arrests."

"Exactly what were you doing in the middle of that operation, anyway?" Leahy asked suddenly. "You were way out of channels, weren't you?"

Nick almost laughed. He'd obviously been dead on-target about Leahy's bureaucratic inclinations. He wondered if the agent was trying to put together a flow chart.

"Yeah, Agent Leahy, I was way out of channels," he agreed and saw the other agent grimace. He gave the Oliver-Leahy partnership a very low chance of survival. "I was *asked* to go way out of channels."

"By whom?"

"By a friend."

"Does this 'friend' have a name?" While the question clearly was intended to be sarcastic, it came out sounding more snotty than anything else.

Nick looked at Al Kozlow, who was regarding Leahy distastefully. After a few seconds, the older man glanced at him and shrugged his permission to drop the bombshell.

Nick casually named the name.

Hayley caught her breath, recognizing it instantly.

"The Deputy Director of the—?" Leahy choked.

Nick showed his teeth. "That was his title the last time I checked." He turned toward Hayley, who was staring at him as though he'd suddenly sprouted an extra head. "I told you some of my friends were marginally respectable," he reminded her, fighting down an urge to reach out for her.

"So you did," she agreed faintly. Then she recalled the "buddy" he'd mentioned phoning earlier. She glanced toward the kitchen. "Was that who—"

Nick nodded.

"Your connection with him isn't in the files," Leahy complained, apparently oblivious to the byplay.

"Alert the media," Oliver suggested, then snorted contemptuously.

"Huh?" His partner turned toward him, clearly taken aback.

"What Agent Oliver is trying to say, Agent Leahy," Al Kozlow translated sardonically, "is that a lot of things that should be in the files aren't, while a lot of things that shouldn't be are. Is that about right, Agent Oliver?"

"Damn straight."

Nick raked a hand back through his hair, suddenly losing patience. "Look, let's cut to the chase, all right? The federal government isn't trailing around snapping pictures of de Sante with miniature cameras just because he looks great in a dinner jacket. What's he up to?"

Dead silence.

Hayley saw Nick's mouth flatten and came to an awful conclusion. They don't know, she thought, appalled.

"You don't know," he said after several seconds, interpreting the lack of response. He glanced from Oliver to Leahy then back to Oliver.

"We don't know," the latter affirmed.

"Any guesses? Educated, ignorant, or otherwise?"

"We think he's going to be brokering some kind of information for someone in the Mideast sometime within the next week," Leahy offered with a hint of defensiveness.

"Oh, that *really* narrows the field."

"O'Neill," Al Kozlow growled warningly, reining in his subordinate for the first time since this episode had started.

"Look," Oliver said tightly, "we have squat—okay? But with de Sante's record, you can bet he isn't selling Girl Scout cookie recipes to some sheik. The word is that whatever this is, de Sante's handling it directly. And you know as well as I do that's anything but standard operating procedure with him. Maybe this is some kind of personal thing. Then again, maybe he's just getting arrogant after two decades of giving us the finger and getting away with it. In any case, de Sante's been in the country for a little over twenty-four hours. You and Miss Jerome are the first people he's had any kind of meaningful contact with."

"As far as you know," Nick amended trenchantly.

"As far as we know," the agent conceded. "These pictures went down the line to the central computer overnight and your face rang some bells. Hell, it rang fire alarms all over town! Now I, for one, happen to believe last night's scene with de Sante happened just the way you and Miss Jerome say it did. And this Michael Becker story is too bizarre not to be true. I know your reputation. If you were going to go dirty, you'd do it with no muss, no fuss, no mention of Tierra del Fuego. And you'd be damned sure to keep your lady friend out of it."

There was a pause. Hayley bit her lip, feeling her cheeks heat once again.

"Yeah," Nick concurred finally. He leaned forward and scooped up a handful of the black-and-white surveillance pictures. Scanning them with a professional eye, he experienced a renewal of the anger he'd felt at the risk Hayley had taken when she'd decided to deal herself into the game with de Santa. Still, he had to admit that she looked as convincing as hell in these photographs. And there was no misinterpreting the expression on de Sante's face. The man was intrigued.

"That thing by de Sante's elbow in a couple of the pictures freaked some of our people pretty good at first," Oliver observed.

Hayley leaned toward Nick, eyeing the photographs he was holding. She found the grainy, oddly angled images unnerving. Had she really looked like that the evening before? she wondered uneasily, not at all sure she wanted to recognize the woman in the pictures as herself.

"You mean his cigarette case?" she questioned after a few seconds.

"I guess he doesn't know smoking's dangerous to his health," Leahy observed with heavy-handed humor.

Acutely conscious of Hayley's increased proximity, Nick shifted slightly, then glanced at the agent. "I'd guess he does and that's one of the reasons why he does it."

"He makes a point of enjoying his vices," Hayley commented with a small shiver. She knit her fingers together.

"How do you know that?" Oliver asked sharply.

"He told me," Hayley answered simply. "I made a comment about the cigarette case when he took it out. It's enameled gold. He has a matching lighter."

"You always pick up on stuff like that?" Leahy queried suspiciously.

"Jerome is an analyst," Al Kozlow inserted. "She sees and she thinks. Now, judging by some of the things I've heard here, I may wonder if she'd thinking very clearly these days. But, yeah. She picks up on stuff like that, Agent Leahy. She picks up on it all the time. Just because she works behind a desk and not out in the field doesn't mean she sits on her brains."

Hayley was startled by—and grateful for—this unsolicited testimonial. But she knew she needed to deal with the implications of Leahy's question herself.

"I noticed the case because it was so unusual," she explained slowly. "It looks like something by Fabergé. And it's obviously very expensive. I...I thought the woman I was pretending to be would probably respond to something like that."

"The Michelle Beckers of the world measure a man by the size of his bank account," Nick added.

"But what was the bit about enjoying his vices?" Oliver pursued, watching Hayley.

She gestured. "As I said, I commented on the case when he took it out and asked if I minded if he smoked. I told him no. After he lit up, he made a quip about how Americans seem to be reverting to Puritanism—no smoking, no drinking, no rich foods, and so forth. He said he preferred to indulge himself."

"Was this before or after he ordered the most expensive bottle of champagne the club had in stock?"

Hayley blinked. "Before."

"In other words, if this guy was a junkie he'd probably shoot up with a sterling silver syringe?" Leahy suggested.

"Actually, he used to carry pharmaceutical grade cocaine in a solid gold vial," Nick said.

Oliver gave him a sharp look. "Do you think he might be powdering the inside of his nose on a regular basis?"

Nick understood Oliver's concern. While cocaine addiction might make a man vulnerable, it also tended to make him paranoid and extremely unpredictable. He shook his head decisively, then answered, "The snow was mostly for show four years ago. Part of his image. And the ladies loved it."

Special Agent Leahy leaned forward in his seat. He cleared his throat significantly. "Speaking of ladies—"

"No," Nick cut in flatly. "Forget about it."

"Nick—"

Nick's eyes sliced to his boss. "No way, Al. She's an amateur."

"But she handled herself like a pro last night, O'Neill," Oliver pointed out. "You said so yourself."

Hayley had stiffened when Nick had interrupted Agent Leahy. She went absolutely rigid now, her gaze bouncing back and forth between the four men. Dear God, she thought, her stomach lurching. They're talking about *me!*

"She took a hell of a chance and she got lucky," Nick countered harshly. "I'm not going to let her run that kind of risk again."

Hayley stared. *He* wasn't going to let *her*—?

"But if there's a chance de Sante might let something slip—"

"For God's sake!" Nick clenched his hands, wondering if Leahy could possibly be as naive as he sounded. "Men like de Sante don't let anything slip to anybody. And they sure as hell don't talk shop with high class hookers! If you're going to send somebody on a fishing expedition, send me. Send Neil James."

"De Sante doesn't trust Neil James," Oliver noted softly.

"So?" Nick challenged. His voice was cold. So were his eyes. "Neil James doesn't trust him, either. That's the way it works. You know that, Oliver, even if your partner here doesn't."

"But if she could help—" it was Leahy again.

"*She* has a name," Hayley snapped suddenly, unable to stay silent any longer. "And *she* would appreciate it if all of *you* would stop talking about her as though she wasn't sitting right here!"

"Hayley—" Nick began.

"Jerome—" Al Kozlow rumbled.

"That's better," she said tartly. Then she turned her head and looked at the two FBI agents. "I take it you're interested in having me go undercover as Michelle Becker?"

"You take it right," Oliver confirmed immediately.

Goaded by impulses she didn't really understand, Hayley lifted her chin with a trace of defiance, her fair hair rippling back from her face.

"When do I start?" she asked.

Ten

"**Y**ours, hers, or someplace else?" the government agent masquerading as a chauffeur asked in a flat voice.

Nick glanced at Hayley, who was seated to his right. While she was close enough so he could touch her by simply stretching out his hand, she was cloaked in an aura of aloofness that made her seem very far away. Her head was tilted back and her long lashes veiled her eyes. She gave no indication she'd heard the driver's question.

Damn this job, Nick thought savagely.

"Hers," he said aloud, keeping his voice steady.

"You got it," came the uninflected reply.

Nick closed his eyes as the limousine he and Hayley were riding in eased away from the curb in front of one of Manhattan's finest hotels. They—or, rather, Neil James and Michelle Becker—had just finished dropping off Philippe de Sante and a stunningly voluptuous redhead named Vanessa after a night on the town. The evening's encounter had been a success in so far as their covers were still intact. Beyond that . . .

Beyond that, Nick didn't much care at this point. Yes, he wanted to see de Sante go down and stay down. But not if it meant putting Hayley in jeopardy. If it came to a choice between popping the Frenchman and protecting Hayley, he wouldn't hesitate for a heartbeat.

He inhaled deeply, catching the elusively provocative scent of Hayley's perfume and the warm, womanly fragrance of her skin. His hands clenched of their own volition. So did the muscles in his belly.

He wanted to reach for her. To draw her into his arms and taste the sweetness of her mouth once more. He wanted to hear her gasp his name on a shattered breath and feel her coming apart in his hands as he brought her to the brink of—

Stop it! Nick ordered himself, opening his eyes.

He shifted abruptly, acutely aware of the hot, heavy throb of arousal between his thighs. He ached. God, how he ached! It had become a painfully familiar feeling during the past several days. But he knew he couldn't seek the balm he so urgently needed as long as he and Hayley were working as a team. He was disturbed enough by the erotic memories of what had happened Saturday night and Sunday morning. He couldn't afford to have his mind any more clouded than it already was.

He had to stay detached. Undistracted. He *had* to.

But once this job was over...

Nick exhaled in carefully controlled increments. When he thought his discipline would hold, he glanced to his right again. He saw Hayley's forehead furrow suddenly and her features tighten.

"Are you all right?" he asked with quiet intensity.

Nick's voice affected Hayley like an intimate caress. Something deep inside her quivered at the rough velvet sound of it. She fought to keep her response from showing on her face.

Are you all right?

No. She wasn't all right. She was caught in a maelstrom of complex and contradictory feelings she couldn't identify or understand, much less control. What was worse, the one person she sensed might be able to help her tame the emotional storm that had overturned her carefully ordered existence was the very person who'd triggered it.

Are you all right?

Dear Lord, how could she be all right when she'd fallen in love with a man who was totally wrong for her? A man she'd known from the instant she'd laid eyes on him would do nothing but wreak havoc in her life if she let him? And she *had* let him! She'd let him and there was a part of her that was wild to go *on* letting him.

Only he hadn't given her any indication that he wanted any more from her than he'd already had. Not once during the past two and a half days had she seen the faintest hint of the lover who'd ravished her senses and her soul with such ecstatic tenderness. Except for this evening, when he'd been playing Neil James to her Michelle Becker, Nick had held her at arm's length, treating her with something very close to indifference.

Hayley drew a shaky breath. She couldn't—wouldn't—allow the man sitting to her left to see the turmoil she was experiencing.

"Hayley?" Nick prompted, watching the uneasy rise and fall of her breasts beneath the bodice of the indigo silk dress she was wearing. For one blood-heating moment, he saw her nipples outlined by the finely woven fabric. His throat went dry and tight. He battled to keep his expression neutral.

Slowly, Hayley turned her head and looked at him. She wondered if her cheeks were as pale as they felt.

"I'm fine, Nick," she said steadily, searching his angular face for some clue about what he was thinking. She saw an expression she couldn't interpret flicker through the depths of his penetrating gray-green eyes. "I'm just a little tired."

"Tired," he repeated slowly, gauging the signs of weariness in her face. He'd tried to warn her—to warn Al and the two FBI men—about the stress of playing an undercover role. Hayley had sailed through her first meeting with de Sante on instinct and adrenaline, not really considering the implications of what she was doing. Tonight, however, she'd had to face the situation fully aware of the risks she was running. Although she'd handled her part flawlessly from start to finish, he understood what the effort had cost her. The strain of having to filter every word and action through an assumed personality could be dangerously debilitating.

Hayley started to manufacture a yawn, then succumbed to the real thing. "Sommmmmmm—uh, excuse me—some lady of the evening I make," she said eventually, striving for a flippant tone and almost achieving it.

Nick glanced at his watch. "Well, considering that it's nearly three in the morning..." His gaze sluiced over her.

Hayley's pulse seemed to stutter for an instant. "Is it that late?"

His mouth twisted. "And getting later all the time."

A few seconds of silence slipped by. Nick reached up and loosened his tie, then unbuttoned the top of his shirt. Hayley moistened her lips and lowered her lashes, trying not to think about the greedy speed with which she'd undone a similar garment three nights before. Her palms and fingertips tingled with the memory of what it had felt like to winnow through the springy thicket of Nick's chest hair, then chart the muscled ridges and rippling sinew beneath.

She crossed her legs, conscious of the silken friction of her dress against her skin. "Shouldn't we report in?" she asked, astonished that her voice sounded fairly close to normal.

"Yeah," Nick agreed tersely, nodding. "Good idea." He leaned forward and snapped the car phone from its cradle, then swiftly punched in a sequence of numbers. He heard a hum of static then a series of whirring noises. Finally there was a click of connection followed by a single ring.

"Oliver's Pizza," a male voice announced.

"What happened to Kozlow's Knishes?"

"O'Neill?"

"Yeah."

"Anything?"

"De Sante's definitely going out of town tomorrow."

"Did he say where he's heading?"

"Oh, yeah. He handed me a printed itinerary."

"I take it that's a no."

"That's a no, Oliver. What's going on? You haven't turned up any airline reservations?"

"Zip. I figure de Sante's going to grab a shuttle to Washington."

Nick was inclined to figure the same thing and said as much. Then he added, "I have a hunch it's going to be a short trip."

"Oh?" Oliver's tone sharpened. "Why?"

"He asked for Michelle Becker's telephone number tonight."

"Which his old buddy Neil James was only too happy to give him."

"Yeah. Right." Nick began massaging the back of his neck. "I didn't get the impression he plans to rack up any long distance charges using it."

"Well, we've got the line and the answering machine hooked up. If de Sante calls, he's going to hear Ms. Becker inviting him to leave a message at the beep. Anything else?"

"No."

"How's your partner holding up?"

Nick slanted another glance at Hayley. She was watching him warily, her fair brows veed together, her soft lower lip caught between the serrated edges of her white teeth. He experienced a rush of emotion—passion, possessiveness, protectiveness—so fierce he had to look away.

"She's fine," he said roughly, his fingers tightening around the phone. "I'm taking her home right now."

"Get some sleep, O'Neill."

"Yeah. You, too, Oliver."

The limousine came to a halt in front of Hayley's building less than a minute later.

"Wait here," Nick instructed the driver. "I won't be staying."

"Whatever you say," the other man returned with a shrug.

Hayley registered Nick's words with a pang. Logic told her they shouldn't hurt, but they did. It didn't matter that she hadn't expected—*didn't want!*—him to come upstairs with her. His rejection still cut to the quick.

Yet she trembled when his fingers closed briefly around hers as he handed her out of the car.

And she trembled again when she felt the press of his palm against the small of her back as he guided her across the sidewalk to the entrance of her building. Shimmering ribbons of yearning uncoiled within her, twining around her nervous system.

She bought herself a few seconds by opening her purse and searching for her keys. She extracted them with fumbling movement, then forced herself to look up at Nick.

"So," she said after a moment or two. "Now we wait?"

Nick nodded slowly, his gaze moving over her fair, up-turned face. The urge to reach out and touch was very, very strong. He tried to tell himself he'd be content just to trace the curve of her cheek or to tease the gossamer tendrils that drifted around her hairline, but he knew it wasn't true. If he touched, he would want to take, and if he took . . .

He couldn't. Not yet. Not until this job was over. And not until he and Hayley had had the talk they should have had long before Al Kozlow and the FBI had shown up.

"Now we wait," he echoed flatly.

Hayley swallowed, shaken by the harshness she thought she heard in Nick's tone and the shuttered hostility she thought she read in his face. This was the man she knew more intimately than any other in the world. Yet at this moment, she felt as though he was a total stranger.

"Do you think de Sante will call me?" she questioned finally.

"I think he'll call Michelle Becker," Nick responded. "You were very convincing." His mouth twisted as he suddenly remembered something. "I'll try to be the same this evening."

Hayley blinked, not understanding his last comment. "This evening—?" she started, then broke off on a gasp as she realized what Nick was talking about. *"My mother!"*

"And Michael Becker."

Hayley closed her eyes, feeling as though the ground was giving way beneath her feet. She'd forgotten. In the emotional chaos of the past few days, she'd actually *forgotten* about her mother, Michael Becker, and "Operation Mr. Wrong."

"Oh, God," she groaned, then opened her eyes. "Nick, we can't—"

"Yes," he interrupted, "we can."

She shook her head. "But we haven't—"

"Yes, we have."

She stared up at him, totally confused. "You . . . you still want to go through with it?" she asked, unable to hide her disbelief.

"Yes," Nick answered honestly. "I do."

The restaurant where "Operation: Mr. Wrong" was supposed to culminate some fifteen hours later was the epitome of low-key, upper East Side elegance. It was not the kind of place where pleasantly plump women in shocking pink ruffles greeted their daughters with squeals and squeezes.

At least, it wasn't *usually* that kind of place.

"Oh, Hayley . . . Hayley," Pamela Delaney Jerome Martinez de la Madrid Touissante Pynchley-Smythe Horowitz soon-to-be Parker exclaimed delightedly, hugging her daughter for the third time. "I am *so* happy to see you, dear!"

"And I'm happy to see you, too," Hayley responded, returning the embrace with less exuberance but equal affection. She wondered fleetingly whether her mother knew—or cared—that they were the focus of several dozen pairs of eyes.

"Now let me take a good look at you," Pamela commanded once she'd finally let go. She cocked her head to one side, her short, silvery-blond curls shimmering in the soft glow from the restaurant's chandeliers. "Oh, you're so beautiful!" she declared, then glanced at the tall, distinguished-looking man standing to her right. "Isn't she beautiful, Elliot?"

"Almost as beautiful as her mother," came the courtly reply.

"Now, Elliot," Pamela protested with a flirtatious laugh and a fluttery little hand gesture. "You shouldn't say things like that."

"Why not?" her fiancé countered, lifting his brows. "It's true."

Another laugh. Another gesture. "What *am* I going to do with you?"

"Marry me next month, I hope."

"Oh, Elliot," Pamela murmured, blushing rosily. After a moment she glanced down at her engagement ring, then looked back up at her fiancé. Elliot smiled. Pamela smiled back.

For the first time in her life, Hayley had the unmistakable sense that her mother had completely forgotten about her.

"Darling," Elliot Parker said after a few moments, his voice huskier than it had been the last time he'd spoken. Clearing his throat, he glanced at Hayley, obviously trying to gauge her reaction. While there was a faint tinge of embarrassment in his expression, the overwhelming impression Hayley got was of a man who was proudly and profoundly in love and who knew his feelings were reciprocated.

Pamela blinked like a person emerging from a hypnotic trance, then laughed apologetically. "I'm sorry, Hayley. But I'm sure you know how it is when you're—" She stopped abruptly. "Why, where's Michael?" she asked, her brow pleating. "He didn't have to leave town, did he, dear?"

There was no irony in the inquiry. No hint that the soon-to-be Mrs. Elliot Parker was beginning to entertain doubts about the existence of her daughter's alleged lover. There was nothing but maternal concern in her voice, nothing but loving anxiety in her eyes.

Hayley's throat closed up. She felt her cheeks grow pink, then turn pale. She recognized, with an awful sense of shame, that her mother would believe anything she chose to

...ay about Michael Becker—including that he'd packed his ...ags and left for Tierra del Fuego fifteen minutes before.

"Hayley?" Pamela questioned.

"Ah—ah—" Hayley stammered. She couldn't do it, she ...ealized. She simply couldn't lie anymore. "Mother, look, ...have to—"

"Michael *is* going to be here, isn't he?" her mother ...ressed.

"Well—uh—yes, but—"

"Wonderful."

"No." Hayley shook her head vehemently. "It's *not* ...onderful."

She had to stop this. She had to stop this right now. And ...he had to stop Nick! They'd planned to come here to-...ether, but he'd gotten shanghaied into a last-minute meet-...ng with a federal prosecutor, so he'd told her that he'd meet ...er at the restaurant instead. Once he showed up...

No. *No!* She couldn't let that happen!

"Don't look so upset, dear," her mother cooed. "It's ...erfectly all right if Michael's a little late. Good heavens, ...'ve already waited nearly four months to meet him. A few ...nore minutes isn't going to hurt."

"But, Mother—"

"Why don't we all sit down?" Elliot interpolated ...moothly.

"Oh, yes, of course," Pamela agreed, favoring her fi-...ancé with a beaming smile of approval. Then she turned to ...er daughter and prompted, "Hayley? Dear? Wouldn't you ...ike to sit down?"

Hayley swallowed convulsively, knowing what she'd really ...ike to do was to bolt for the door. "Yes," she answered ...aintly. "Yes...of course."

It took them a minute to get settled. Several more min-...ites ticked away while a waiter bustled up to open and pour ...he bottle of champagne Elliot had ordered prior to Hay-...ey's arrival. Although the man performed his task with ef-...iciency and élan, Hayley was on the verge of screaming at ...nim to go away by the time he finally finished and moved ...on.

"Mmm," Pamela sighed after taking a long, savoring sip of the sparkling wine. "Delicious."

Hayley leaned forward to speak, to tell the truth, to try to explain. She opened her lips, but nothing came out.

"Isn't it delicious, Elliot?" Pamela asked, smiling fondly at her fiancé.

"Wonderful, Pamela," he concurred. They clinked their glasses together.

"Mother—"

"Dear, you're not drinking your champagne," her mother chided gently. "This is supposed to be a celebration. After all this time, I'm finally going to meet the man who—" She broke off suddenly, staring over Hayley's left shoulder. "Oh, my," she breathed wonderingly. A delicate hint of color rouged her cheeks, and her eyes began to dance. "Oh, my...yes."

Oh, no, Hayley thought desperately. Out of the corner of her eye, she saw Elliot start to get up from his seat. There was something very odd about his expression. Quaking inwardly, she forced herself to turn in her chair and look.

What she saw was a tall, dark, and potently attractive man dressed in an immaculately tailored charcoal gray suit. His expression exuded intelligence and charm. His manner was the essence of masculine self-assurance. Only the predatory power of his stride and the challenging intensity of his gaze hinted that it might be dangerous to rely too heavily on his aura of civilized sophistication.

Hayley's lips shaped a name. It contained one syllable, not two.

The man who bore that single-syllable name reached their table. Bending, he dropped a quick but claiming kiss on Hayley's mouth.

"I'm sorry I'm late, angel," Nick said softly, his warm breath fanning her skin for an instant. Then he straightened and looked at the two other people at the table. "I'm Michael Becker," he announced calmly, his voice low and resonant. "I hope I haven't kept you waiting too long."

"Not at all, Michael," Pamela assured him, extended her hand. "I'm Hayley's mother. Please, call me Pamela."

Nick took the proffered hand, his mouth curving into a smile that managed to be both respectful and roguish. Hayley watched, stunned, as the color in her mother's cheeks deepened.

"Pamela," Nick said.

"And this is my fiancé—"

"Congressman Parker," Nick completed smoothly, releasing Pamela's hand and offering his own to the older man.

Hayley's gaze bounced from her mother to her future stepfather. He looked tense. After a short but unmistakable hesitation, he clasped Nick's hand and shook it.

"You have quite a memory for names, Mr. Becker," he said evenly.

"It's a necessity in my job, sir," Nick answered.

"Indeed."

"Elliot, darling, sit down and stop looking so serious," Pamela urged gaily. "And you, Michael. You sit down, too. Have some champagne. As I was just telling Hayley—this is a celebration!"

No, Hayley contradicted silently. This is an unmitigated nightmare!

But there was nothing she could do to stop it. Nothing, at least, that wouldn't shatter her mother into a million pieces.

The most horrible thing was that she'd known. From the very beginning she'd known that Nick O'Neill couldn't be trusted. Dear Lord, the man had virtually spelled out his manipulative intentions for her!

"Why do I have this nagging suspicion that I'm being conned into something?" she'd asked him that fateful Saturday morning two and a half weeks before.

"Because you have terrific instincts," he'd responded.

Hayley's stomach roiled.

Terrific instincts, hah!

If her instincts were so terrific, why hadn't she guessed that the man who'd promised he'd help her by pretending to be Mr. Wrong would betray her by pretending to be Mr. Right?

And why hadn't she guessed that she'd betray herself and everything she believed in by wishing that his treacherous pretense could be transformed into reality?

Nick had known Hayley would be angry. He just hadn't known how angry. But even if he had known, he had a gut-level hunch he would have done what he did in the restaurant anyway.

Her temper broke after dinner, in her apartment. They'd ended up there because her mother had voiced a desire to see the place. Everything had proceeded serenely until Pamela and Elliot had made their exit.

And then:

"How...could...you?" Hayley demanded through gritted teeth, her hands fisted, her eyes shooting sapphire flames. She was shaking with rage and hurt and a dozen other emotions. "How *could* you?"

"Hayley, please." Nick took a step forward, she took two steps back. He stopped moving, warned off by the expression on her face. "If you'll just let me try to explain—"

"Explain?" Outrage shredded her voice. "Don't you mean just let you try to lie your way out of this the same way you lied your way into it?"

Nick flinched, recognizing she had every right to accuse him. He'd been dishonest with her almost from the very beginning. But, dammit, there had been no other way to get through her defenses!

"Angel—"

"Don't call me that!" Her rejection of the endearment was unequivocal.

Nick sucked in a breath, fighting for control. "Hayley, I didn't mean to lie—" he began tightly.

"Didn't you?" she flung the question at him like a gauntlet, challenging him to disagree. "You said you'd help me, Nick. You said you'd pretend to be Michael Becker!"

"I *did* pretend to be Michael Becker."

"But not the way we practiced. Not the way we rehearsed. You were supposed to be a horrible person to ight! You were supposed to be a mother-in-law's worst nightmare! But instead you were—were—you w-were—''

Hayley broke off and turned away as she heard her voice start to quaver. Her throat tightened, making it almost impossible to swallow. She blinked rapidly, trying to deny the implications of the sudden stinging at the corners of her eyes.

I'm *not* going to cry, she told herself fiercely, biting down on the inside of her cheek so hard she drew blood. Not now. Not in front of him.

Nick crossed to Hayley in three lithe strides, catching her by the upper arms and spinning her back to face him. "What was I?" he demanded urgently. "What was I tonight?"

"You know," she answered thickly, jerking free of his hands. Even now, even after what he'd done, the touch of his hands made her body stir and her blood sing. She backed away, steeling herself against the physical responses he evoked. "You know what you were."

"I was myself, Hayley. Nothing more, nothing less."

"Yourself?" she shook her head, the impulse to weep subsiding. "You don't have a 'self,' Nick. You've got a grab bag of them! You change your personality the way most people change their socks."

"That's not true," he denied sharply.

"Yes, it is!" she insisted. "I've seen you. In the office—"

"Dammit, that's work! Undercover is what I do. It's not what I am."

"What about during the two weeks you were on vacation?"

"What about it?"

"You were like a—a—" she gestured "—like a chameleon!"

"And you weren't?" he flashed back. "My God, Hayley. You matched me change for change, personality for personality!'

"No." The word came out on a gasp.

"Yes."

She shook her head again, her fair hair belling out around her neck. "I'm not like you, Nick. *I'm not!* I don't set out to con people—"

"Except your mother," he inserted trenchantly, his temper stretched right to the breaking point.

"That—" she almost choked on what he was suggesting. "That's different!"

"How?"

"I've told you!"

Once again, Nick closed the distance between himself and Hayley. Once again, he caught her by the upper arms. Only this time, when she tried to pull free, he didn't let her go.

"You've told me a lot of things, Hayley," he ground out, finally goaded beyond the limits of good sense and self-discipline. "Now let me tell you something. I did what I did tonight—I lied, I conned, I broke my promise to pretend to be Mr. Wrong—because I wanted your mother to like me. And I wanted her to like me because I love you. Do you hear me? I love you, dammit!"

For one awful moment, Hayley thought she might faint. Her head swam. Her vision blurred. Her legs seemed to turn to jelly.

"No," she denied, closing her eyes. She wouldn't believe it. She *couldn't.*

"Yes," Nick affirmed, alarmed by her sudden pallor. He tightened his grip on her arms. "Hayley—"

She opened her eyes again. Her pupils were so dilated that they nearly obliterated the blue of her irises. "You can't love me," she said. "You *can't.*"

"I can and I do." This was not, Nick acknowledged with a pang, the way he'd intended to tell Hayley how he felt. But perhaps the very crudeness of his confession would help convince her of the truth of his words.

"Why are you doing this to me?" she asked shakily. His declaration had left her defenseless, her nerves flayed, her emotions stripped raw. "Why can't you just leave me alone? I don't want this. I've *never* w-wanted—"

Her words sliced through Nick like a knife. "You wanted this just as much as I—" he began harshly.

"I knew from the very beginning," Hayley went on, unable to stop now that she'd started. "From the moment I met you, I knew I had to stay away from you. I knew if I didn't, you'd turn my life upside down. And I was right! I didn't stay away from you and now my life's so ... so completely mixed up, so ... so totally confused ..." She stared at him, stricken.

"My God," Nick whispered, his fingers going slack. The anger he'd felt only seconds before evaporated as he absorbed what he'd just heard. From the very beginning, she'd said. *From the moment she'd met him.*

Sweet heaven. Could she possibly mean—?

"I don't want you to love me, Nick," Hayley concluded, her voice brittle and her eyes dangerously bright. "And I don't want to love you."

Nick realized he'd been holding his breath. He released it in a rush. The pain he saw in Hayley's face nearly undid him.

"But you do," he asserted when he'd recovered the ability to speak. His voice sounded very strange to him. His heart was hammering so hard he felt as though his rib cage might crack open from the inside. "You may not want to, but you do love me."

"It doesn't matter."

"The hell it doesn't!" Nick reached for her, not quite sure what he meant to do, but desperate to touch her once again.

Hayley evaded his grasp. "I grew up in an emotional earthquake zone, Nick," she told him. "But I survived it. And what I want now—what I *need*—is stability and certainty and a sense that I have some control over my life. I can't have that with you. So whatever I feel ..." Her voice frayed into silence.

"And what about what I feel?" Nick asked after a few jagged moments.

She gestured, the movement of her hands delicate but desolated. "I'm sorry."

"No," he contradicted, shaking his head. "You're not sorry. You're afraid. You've been afraid of me—of yourself—from the very start."

Hayley swallowed convulsively. "If I am, I've got good reason to be."

Nick shook his head again, clenching and unclenching his hands. "You've got *no* reason to be. *I love you,* Hayley. And I'm going to go on loving you. That isn't going to change!"

Hayley lowered her gaze for a moment, biting her lower lip. She'd never dreamed she was capable of enduring such pain. She felt as though her heart was being torn in two. Finally she forced herself to look up at Nick once again.

"I can't take that risk, Nick," she said with desperate, devastating simplicity. "I . . . can't."

In the end, he asked her what she wanted of him, and she answered that she wanted him to leave her alone.

Although the expression in her eyes contradicted her words, he did.

It wasn't until many hours later that he remembered something he'd failed to tell her.

The "something" was that he was virtually certain her future stepfather knew her purported future fiancé was a fake.

Eleven

The following day dawned gray and gloomy, very much in keeping with Hayley's mood.

She got out of bed long before her alarm clock went off. Her eyes were puffy, and her temples throbbed dully. She'd slept very little. To sleep was to dream and to dream was to yearn for what she'd rejected.

Nick, she thought. Oh, God . . . *Nick.*

Hayley showered, dressed, then did her hair and makeup. The process should have been automatic and efficient. Instead, her movements seemed uncoordinated and vaguely out of sync.

Although she'd woken up early, Hayley left her apartment a good fifteen minutes behind her normal schedule. She ended up missing her usual bus and had to resort to taking the subway to the office. Throughout the noisy, underground trip, she kept telling herself over and over that she'd done the right thing—the only thing—the night before. But it didn't ease the pain she was experiencing. She hurt. She hurt so much she could scarcely breathe.

"I love you, Hayley," Nick had said. *"And I'm going to go on loving you. That isn't going to change."*

"I can't take that risk, Nick," she'd replied. *"I...can't."*

Hayley desperately wished she could, but she knew she couldn't. She also knew that—despite everything that had happened—her inability to do so had more to do with her not trusting herself than with not trusting Nick.

The jam-packed subway screeched to a halt at the station she wanted. The doors slid open. She was practically shoved out onto the littered platform by the jostling throng of disembarking passengers.

A minute later she emerged above ground. The autumn air was chilly and vaguely damp. The sky was overcast, even ominous. People scurried by, studiously avoiding eye contact with each other.

Shivering involuntarily, Hayley began trudging toward the massive granite federal building that housed her office. The only thing heavier than her footsteps was her heart.

Nick had been right when he'd accused her of being afraid. She was. She was afraid of her thoughts and feelings, of her wants and needs. She was afraid in ways she hadn't been afraid since she was a child.

She'd been so confident she knew herself so well, saw herself so clearly. Yet she now had to admit that she really hadn't known herself at all. She'd been blind to her true nature. And that, in a sense, was the most frightening thing of all. It was frightening because it meant that she could no longer depend on herself or her reactions.

Hayley wasn't certain she could cope with that.

In fact, she wasn't certain she could cope with much of anything anymore.

Hayley reached her destination. She stopped at the bottom of the stairs that led up to the federal building, her pulse starting to pound, the dull ache in her temples intensifying.

I can't, she thought desperately. I can't face Nick. Or Al. Or anyone else. I *can't.*

But she had to. She had to because whatever her personal problems, she had professional responsibilities she couldn't shirk. Philippe de Sante was still at large and up to something, and she was supposed to be helping to bring him down.

Hayley swallowed hard. Drew a deep breath. Squared her shoulders. Then she marched up the stairs and pushed through one of the three revolving doors that opened into the entrance lobby. After flashing her identification badge at a grim-faced security guard and passing through a metal detector, she took an elevator up to the floor where she worked.

"Mr. Kozlow wants to see you," the receptionist announced as soon as she stepped out of the car.

Hayley felt a frisson of apprehension skitter up her spine but she managed to keep her expression neutral. "Thank you, Diane," she responded quietly, unbuttoning the front of her coat.

"Right now," the woman emphasized.

"I'm on my way."

"You're late, Jerome," Al Kozlow growled at her about thirty seconds later.

"I'm sorry," she answered, smoothing her hair and straightening her glasses. She glanced around uneasily. She'd expected that Nick would be in the office alone with their boss. He wasn't.

"It's not like you to be late."

She made a vague little gesture, unwilling to offer excuses for her tardiness. Where was Nick? she wondered. Half of her felt relieved by his absence. The other half...

She shook her head a little, not wanting to think about what the other half of her was feeling.

Kozlow knit his shaggy, silvery brows, assessing her through narrowed eyes. "Then again, maybe it *is* like you, and you've just been putting on an act these six months," he commented eventually.

Hayley stiffened at the suggestion but said nothing. Her boss had made similar remarks during the past several days. She'd tried to ignore them and their implications as best she could.

Kozlow studied her for a few more seconds, then picked up a file folder from the top of his paper-strewn desk and extended it toward her. After a fractional hesitation, Hayley walked forward to claim it.

"That's the surveillance report on de Sante's overnight jaunt to Washington," he explained sourly as she took the folder from him. "Ten pages of nothing. The latest word is that he's on his way back to—"

The phone on Kozlow's desk shrilled suddenly. He picked it up.

"What?" he demanded brusquely, then paused. Hayley watched him silently, clutching the file to her chest. She saw his features harden and his cheeks flush an ugly brick red.

Nick she thought instantly, a chill of fear running through her. Dear Lord, something's happened to Nick.

Kozlow cursed. "How the hell did that—no. No, don't tell me, Leahy. I don't want to know." He stopped speaking and listened for several seconds. He nodded abruptly. "Yes. He's still registered. We'd better hope that he hasn't realized—what? No. O'Neill's out on the street, putting the touch to some old contacts. Jerome just got in. What? No. Nothing on Michelle Becker." He paused, then concluded sharply, "Fine. I'll be waiting."

And with that, he slammed the receiver back into its cradle.

"What happened?" Hayley questioned anxiously.

Kozlow drummed his stubby fingers against the top of his desk. "De Sante flew in on the shuttle from Washington about thirty minutes ago," he announced grimly. "Our team lost him at LaGuardia."

"Oh, no."

"Oh, yes."

"We don't have any idea where he is?"

"He's still checked in at the hotel where you and O'Neill dropped him off the other night. If what happened at the airport was our side screwing up—not him doing a deliberate shake job—he'll probably go back there eventually. But, in the meantime . . ." Kozlow grimaced and shook his head.

Hayley worried her lower lip with her teeth for a few seconds. "What about the contacts you said Nick was getting in touch with?"

"We'll have to wait and see." Kozlow ran a palm over his balding pate, then questioned, "Are you ready if de Sante calls Michelle Becker?"

Hayley hesitated, then dipped her head. Her hair swung forward to curtain the sides of her face. She brushed it back with two quick swipes of her hands. "Yes," she said.

"Are you sure, Jerome?"

"Very."

There was a pause. Kozlow steepled his fingers, openly scrutinizing her once again.

"Is there anything else?" Hayley asked finally, forcing herself to sustain his gaze.

"Not for now."

"Fine."

She was halfway out the door when Kozlow spoke again.

Hayley checked herself in midstride, stunned by his use of her first name. Slowly, she pivoted. "Yes?" she asked warily.

Her boss shifted in his seat. His expression held a peculiar mix of determination and discomfort. "It's easy to get the wrong idea about O'Neill, you know," he said after a few moments.

Hayley lifted her chin. "It's easy to get the wrong idea about a lot of people, Mr. Kozlow," she responded evenly. Then, after waiting a beat, she turned and left.

The surveillance report on Philippe de Sante's one-day trip to Washington, D.C., was as bad as Al Kozlow had said. Detailed, yes. But dull, dull, dull. It offered no hint of illegal dealings, no whiff of illicit doings. Indeed, the activities it chronicled were so ostentatiously innocent that Hayley couldn't help but wonder whether the Frenchman was aware he was being watched.

She'd just finished reading the report for the second time when the phone on her desk rang. She picked it up with one hand and used the other to push her glasses back into place.

"Extension 2976."

"Hayley?"

She recognized the male on the other end immediately.
"Elliot?"

"Ah . . . yes."

Hayley sat up. There was a quality of constraint in his
tone that raised goose bumps on the back of her neck.

"Is everything all right?" she asked quickly.

No answer.

Hayley's fingers tightened on the phone. A host of possibilities—each one worse than the one before—sluiced
through her mind. "Elliot?"

The sound of a throat being cleared came through the
line. "This is very difficult for me—"

"Is something wrong with my mother?" she interrupted.

"What?" Elliot sounded startled by the question. Then
he recovered and said firmly, "No. Oh, no, Hayley. Pamela—your mother's fine. Just fine. She's out shopping."

"Then why—?"

"Are you free for lunch?"

The apparent invitation threw Hayley off balance.
"Lunch?" she repeated blankly. "Today?"

"Yes. I'd like to speak to you privately."

A pause. Hayley contemplated the implications of what
had just been said, growing more and more uneasy with
each passing moment.

"You mean . . . without my mother?"

"Yes."

"But why?"

Elliot cleared his throat again. "This really isn't something I want to discuss over the phone, Hayley. Could you
possibly join me for lunch? I realize it's last minute and I
know how busy you are, but I've made reservations at a
restaurant near you." He gave her the particulars, then
added persuasively, "Please, say yes."

Hayley moistened her lips. "Elliot—"

"This is important," her mother's fiancé went on. "We
need to talk about your—" he paused as though searching

for the proper word, cleared his throat for the third time, then bluntly concluded ''—about Michael Becker.''

"So, what about Michael Becker?" Hayley asked about two and a half hours later, hoping the inquiry sounded less anxious to her stepfather-to-be than it did to her.

Elliot Parker took a quick drink of the Chenin Blanc he'd ordered to go with their meal. The restaurant he'd selected for this conversation was as famed for the excellence of its cellar as for the extravagance of its cuisine. Under different circumstances, Hayley would have enjoyed the superb food and wine. As it was, she'd left most of what she'd been offered untouched.

Elliot put down his glass. Although he'd eaten and drunk heartily, Hayley had the sense he hadn't cared about what he'd consumed.

"Elliot?" she prompted, unable to soften the edge in her voice.

Her mother's fiancé glanced around, clearly uncomfortable. Hayley found herself wondering if he had the same feeling of being watched that she did. The sensation of being under scrutiny had assailed her shortly after she'd sat down in the banquette seat next to Elliot. At first she'd chalked it up to nerves. Then she'd decided that the unsettling sensation probably stemmed from the mirrors which decorated the restaurant's shimmering peach walls. They bounced reflected images back and forth, making it possible to keep a covert eye on every corner in the place. They created an intimate—but to Hayley's mind, rather oppressive—atmosphere.

Elliot sighed and brought his gaze back to hers. The expression on his craggily handsome face was troubled. "I love your mother very much, Hayley," he declared with quiet but compelling sincerity. "I hope you believe that."

"I do," Hayley replied after a moment, her throat tight. The mention of the word "love" flicked her on the raw. "Seeing the way you look at her...hearing the way you talk to her..." She gestured, unable to continue.

"Yes, well, I don't want you to think that I make a practice of going behind her back. Because I don't. Your mother and I try to be absolutely honest with one another. But in this instance—" Elliot frowned.

"In this instance—what?"

"Pamela was very taken with your friend last night. He completely charmed her."

Hayley flushed. She swallowed hard, trying to dislodge the lump that suddenly threatened to choke her. "Yes. I know."

Elliot leaned forward. "That's why I haven't said anything to her. Because she was so pleased and excited."

"I . . . I don't I understand."

"Hayley, Michael Becker is a fraud," the former congressman stated flatly.

Hayley felt the blood drain out of her cheeks. "Wh-what?"

"The man you're involved with isn't Michael Becker. His name is O'Neill—Nicholas O'Neill. He works for the government. Or, at least, that's who he said he was and what he did when he testified in closed door session before the oversight committee a few years back."

Hayley suddenly remembered the peculiar exchange Nick and Elliot had had when they'd been "introduced" the previous evening.

"Congressman Parker," Nick had said, offering his hand to the older man.

"You have quite a memory for names," Elliot had returned, clasping Nick's hand after a noticeable hesitation.

"It's a necessity in my job, sir," Nick had answered.

"Indeed," had come the tight reply.

Nick had known, she thought with a spurt of anger. Nick had *known* Elliot Parker had recognized him and he hadn't said one word to her! The man who had sworn he loved her had known she was in danger of being exposed to her mother as a liar and he hadn't dropped so much as a hint!

"My first thought when I saw him was that you'd gotten tangled up in some kind of undercover operation through the Justice Department," Elliot continued. "But then I watched the two of you together, and I realized that all the

hings your mother had said about you finally falling in love
were true and so I decided—"

"No," Hayley denied shakily. "Elliot, it's not like that.
'm not—"

And then she glimpsed something in one of the mirrors
ung opposite their table that made her heart lurch and her
breath wedge at the top of her throat.

A man.

He was tall. Silver-haired. Faultlessly dressed.

He was taking an enameled cigarette case from the inner
pocket of his elegantly tailored navy blue suit jacket as he
surveyed the restaurant with heavy-lidded eyes. He looked
utterly at ease. The beginnings of a faintly disdainful smile
tugged at the corners of his thin-lipped mouth.

Hayley knew, to the instant, when Philippe de Sante registered her presence.

She had one brief moment of panic.

She couldn't—

She didn't—

"Hayley?" Elliot questioned worriedly, putting a hand on
her upper arm.

Yes, she could.

Yes, she did.

Hayley turned to her stepfather-to-be, a strange kind of
calm descending on her. She knew exactly what she had to
do and how she had to do it.

"You were right about my having gotten tangled up in
something through the Justice Department, Elliot," she said
steadily, shifting her body nearer to his. He stiffened in
surprise. She stroked the fingers of one hand down his lapel. He stiffened even more, something very close to shock
appearing in his eyes.

"Hayley, what in the name of heaven—" he began.

"I don't have time to explain," she murmured, stroking
her fingers back up his lapel. She ran her tongue over her
lips then offered him the most provocative smile she could
produce. "Please, Elliot. Just follow my lead. The main
thing to remember is that my name is Michelle Becker and
that you're paying me for my company."

Twelve

Nick spotted Hayley coming out of Al Kozlow's office and breathed a quick prayer of thankfulness. Oliver had been right. She hadn't gone for the day, but she was obviously preparing to.

"Hayley!" he called urgently, striding down the hallway toward her.

Hayley went rigid in response to the resonant male voice. Her pulse accelerated. A sudden surge of longing welled up within her, its liquid heat warring with her instinctive stiffening.

The last person in the world she wanted to see at this moment was Nick O'Neill. She knew she would have been hard-pressed to deal with him if she'd been fresh and strong and prepared. But given her current state of mind...

She was still reeling from the impact of the bombshell Elliot Parker had dropped on her at lunch. And when she added to that the surprise encounter with Philippe de Sante followed by the pressure of a lengthy and intense interrogation by Special Agents Oliver and Leahy plus a rather more intimate grilling by Al Kozlow, she had to wonder how much one person could be expected to take without going to pieces.

I'll take what I have to take, she told herself fiercely. I always have. I always will.

"Hayley," Nick repeated, making an effort to moderate his tone as he read the resistance in every line of her posture. For a moment he was genuinely afraid she was going to turn away. But then, just as he reached her, she pivoted to face him.

They confronted each other in silence for several long seconds.

"I saw Oliver downstairs in the lobby," Nick said without preamble. "He told me what happened in the restaurant with de Sante and Parker."

There was a lock of hair curving down over his forehead. Hayley was appalled by the urge she felt to push it back into place. She clenched her hands, her nails biting into her palms.

"Good," she responded coolly, lifting her chin. "If you have any questions, you can read the report I just gave Al."

"I've got a lot of questions and I'd rather ask you," he returned flatly, cataloging the signs of stress in her face. He could see a vein throbbing in her right temple. Her fair skin was paler than normal and pulled taut against the elegant bones of her cheeks and brow. There were bruise-colored smudges beneath her wide blue eyes. She'd chewed off her lipstick, leaving her mouth bare and vulnerable.

Nick remembered the hot, honeyed taste of that ripe, beautifully shaped mouth. He remembered the feel of it opening against his own. His body tightened and he experienced a familiar heaviness between his thighs.

"Too bad," Hayley answered. "Because I'm going home."

Nick extended his hand to touch her. He couldn't stop himself. Only the fact that she instantly backed off a step made him abort the gesture.

"Don't, Nick," she said sharply, shaking her head.

He brought his hand back down to his side, his fingers fisting as he fought for control. Keep it professional, he ordered himself. Keep it professional . . . for now.

"Oliver said your cover as Michelle Becker is intact," he commented after a moment.

"More so than yours as Michael," Hayley retorted, her eyes flashing.

Nick didn't even consider pretending not to understand what she meant by this remark. "Elliot Parker recognized me as Nick O'Neill," he said without inflection.

"He *remembered* you as Nick O'Neill. He *recognized* you as a fraud," Hayley returned, spitting out the verbs as though she found their flavor offensive. "That's why he asked me to lunch today. He wanted to talk to me about you—or should I say Michael Becker?—before he said anything to my mother. He was trying to protect her. He knew she'd be shattered if she found out the man who charmed her so completely last night didn't really exist. But as soon as he'd told me the truth, Philippe de Sante walked in. Which meant I never got a chance to explain. And then afterward, after I got through playing Michelle Becker, I had to lie and say I *couldn't* explain because it was all a matter of national security. I also had to ask him to please go on keeping everything he knows—or thinks he knows—about me and you a secret from my mother."

Pain clouded Hayley's sky-colored eyes. The sight of that pain, much more than her deliberately hurtful words, tore at Nick's heart.

God, he thought bitterly. How had things gotten so horribly out of hand . . . gone so totally wrong? He loved Hayley. And he knew she loved him, for all that it seemed to terrify her. Wasn't love supposed to bring people together, not build barriers between them? *Wasn't it?*

He had to get through to her. He had to find a way to ease her fears about herself. Her fears about him. Her fears about the two of them together. He also had to set right the mistakes he'd made.

"Hayley, please—" he began, his determined professionalism of just a few moments before discarded.

"Why didn't you tell me you knew Elliot knew you weren't Michael Becker?" she cut in, her voice rising. "Why didn't you say something?"

"I didn't have a chance."

"You had *every* chance!"

"I had more important things to say to you, dammit!"

"More important in whose opinion?"

"In my opinion!"

"Well, I didn't want to hear any of them!"

"That doesn't change the fact that you needed to—"

At that moment the door to Al Kozlow's office swung open with a bang.

"What the *hell* is going on out here?" the older man demanded, stomping out into the hallway. His face and scalp were flushed and his voice was as abrasive as steel wool. He skewered Nick with a look, then glared at Hayley, "I thought you were heading home, Jerome," he snapped.

Furious words of explanation and self-justification trembled on the tip of Hayley's tongue. It nearly choked her to swallow them. She sliced an angry, accusatory glance at Nick, then transferred her attention back to Kozlow.

"I was," she finally managed to reply. Her tone was as rigid as her spine.

"So, get out of here," her boss said with a brusque gesture. "If there's anything to report after Oliver gets done talking to your mother's fiancé, I'll let you know. And you'll be the second to find out if de Sante phones Michelle Becker."

After a second or two, Hayley dipped her head. Her temples were pounding. Her blood was roaring in her ears. She felt more than a little sick. "Fine," she acquiesced tightly, then turned on her heel and walked away.

Nick opened his mouth to speak her name. To stop her.

"Let her go, O'Neill," Kozlow said harshly. "I want your butt in here now." And with that, he wheeled around and marched back into his office.

Al was ordering—not asking—and Nick knew it. He also knew that while his superior had cut him a lot of slack on a lot of different occasions, he wasn't about to do so in this particular instance.

Nick waited just long enough to see Hayley disappear around the corner at the end of the hall, then did as he'd been commanded.

"Shut the door and sit down," Kozlow instructed tersely, settling himself heavily behind his desk.

Again, Nick followed orders.

There was a lengthy silence. Finally Kozlow exhaled on a frustrated hiss. He leaned forward, steepling his fingers on the top of his desk, then asked very quietly, "Can you give me one good reason why I shouldn't yank you off the de Sante case?"

Nick remained absolutely still. "Aside from the fact that I'll quit?" he responded, deliberately matching the other man's tone.

"Threat?"

"Promise."

"Because you want de Sante or because you want—" Kozlow nodded his balding head toward the hallway "—her?"

Nick let a few seconds tick by. "What do you think?" he countered when he thought he could trust his voice. He knew from a sudden flickering in his boss's eyes that he hadn't waited long enough.

"I think you're professional enough to know that when things get personal, people get hurt," Kozlow said, answering the question in his own unique fashion.

The muscles of Nick's stomach knotted. "I'm not going to let Hayley get hurt, Al," he replied softly. "Not by de Sante. Not by the FBI. Not by anyone."

"Including you?"

The knot in his gut got tighter. "Including me."

There was another silence. Eventually Kozlow's posture relaxed a little. He eased back in his chair. "How long have I known you, O'Neill?" he inquired.

Nick forked the fingers of one hand through his hair. "Twenty-one years come March."

The older man nodded, his expression reflective. "That was some wedding...your mother and Deke."

Nick knew this sudden detour down Memory Lane had a purpose. He just wasn't certain what it was. "Yeah."

"I told Deke I thought he was getting a treasure in Anne and a truckload of trouble in you."

Nick wasn't offended by this blunt statement. He was well aware of how uncomplimentary Al's initial assessment of him had been. All things considered, he didn't think that assessment had been very far off the mark.

"That's the best man's prerogative, isn't it?" he responded. "Giving advice to the groom?"

"Unwanted advice. Deke told me he knew he was going to have problems with you. But he also told me you had real potential." Kozlow shook his head. "He's a tough son a bitch, but he's got better instincts than any cop I've ever worked with."

Nick's mouth twisted. "Yeah, well, it was Deke's toughness—not his instincts—that first got through to me."

"What was that line he used to use on you?"

"'Kid, I don't give a damn about rehabilitating you. I just want to redirect your energies.'"

"Right." Kozlow shifted awkwardly. He paused for a few moments, obviously weighing his words and finding many of them wanting. Finally he resumed speaking. "Look, O'Neill, you've been playing games most of your life—"

"I'm not playing now, Al," Nick interrupted. "What's going on between Hayley and me may have started out as a game, but it isn't now."

"No conning?"

"No conning." Nick's voice was very steady, as though he were making a pledge. "Not her. Not myself. Not anymore."

Nick saw something—satisfaction?—in his boss's eyes. Kozlow said nothing for several seconds, then nodded abruptly. "Okay, then," he growled.

"Okay, then—*what?*"

"Okay, then, you just gave me a damned good reason for not yanking you off the de Sante case." Suddenly Kozlow was all business. "Speaking of which, do you have anything to report?"

Nick accepted the graceless change of topic without protest. He knew protesting wouldn't do him any good. Al had said his piece and that was all there was to it.

"Nothing except we're not the only ones wondering what de Sante's up to," he answered flatly. "The speculation is that it's something personal. And since 'personal' isn't de Sante's style, a lot of people are nervous."

Kozlow snorted. "Misery loves company. Well, write it up. And once you've finished your report, go home. *Home,* O'Neill. Don't chase after Jerome. Not tonight."

Nick got to his feet. He said nothing.

"That's an order," Al added.

"I figured." Nick turned and headed toward the door. He was reaching for the knob when his boss spoke his name. His *first* name.

He pivoted back. "What?"

"I just wanted to say that it was nice of you to visit your mother while you were on vacation."

"It was nice of you to let her know I was on vacation."

The older man gestured. "I gave Deke a call. Maybe it was a good idea. Maybe it wasn't." He paused for several moments, then finally asked, "Did you say anything to them about . . . Hayley?"

One corner of Nick's mouth kicked up in rueful recollection. "My mother's a reformed con artist. Deke's a retired cop. I didn't have to. They took one look at my face and they figured out everything but her name."

Hayley had decided she had two options.

She could cry . . .

Or she could clean.

She was down on her hands and knees scrubbing her kitchen floor when the security intercom buzzed. Her head jerked up and her fingers spasmed at the sound.

Nick! she thought, her heart leaping into her throat. She sat back on her heels.

She wasn't going to answer it. She *wasn't.*

The intercom buzzed again.

Hayley bit her lower lip, listening to the insistent sound. There was something almost hysterical about the continued shrilling. Nick was a great many things, but hysterical was not one of them.

Apprehension touched her with clammy fingers, sending nasty shivers scurrying up and down her spine.

Bzzz.

Slowly, shakily, Hayley got to her feet. She wiped her hands on the pullover top of the gray sweat suit she'd put on, then walked out into her foyer.

Bzzzzz—

She pressed the Talk button on the intercom panel. "Hello?"

"H-H-Hayley?"

"Mother?" Hayley gasped, instantly recognizing the tear-choked voice. Something had to be terribly, terribly wrong. For all her emotionalism, Pamela Delaney Jerome Martinez de la Madrid Touissante Pynchley-Smythe Horowitz was not a crier.

"Y-yes. I n-need to... to... talk to you."

Hayley hit the Enter button.

Pamela sobbed stormily into a fistful of sodden tissues.

"Mother, *please,*" Hayley pleaded, stroking her mother's heaving shoulders. They were sitting side by side on her living room sofa. Or, rather, she was sitting and her mother was huddled into a pathetic heap. "Tell me what's wrong. I can't help you if I don't know what's wrong."

"No-nobody c-can help m-m-me."

"That's not true!" Hayley disputed quickly, shocked by the despairing tone in her mother's assertion. "Whatever it is—"

Pamela lifted her head. "It's Elliot."

"Elliot?" Hayley echoed, shock giving way to alarm.

Her mother nodded and sniveled loudly.

"What about Elliot?"

"He... he... there's s-s-someone else, Hayley. We're n-not even m-m-married and he... he's already b-being unfaithful. At least . . . at least J-Jean Luc waited until after the w-wedding!''

"No!" Hayley shook her head vehemently.

Pamela blinked, blotting her runny nose with the tissues she was holding. She sniveled again. "Oh, yes. Jean Luc h-had a m-mistress—"

"Not Jean Luc!" Hayley practically exploded. *"El-liot!"*

Her mother's face crumpled. She started to sob. "He...he has one, t-too! A m-mistress, I mean. And sh-she's young enough—young enough to b-be his d-d-daughter! Oh, Hayley. Elliot's the f-first m-man since your father who's made me...made me f-feel..." Pamela's ability to speak dissolved in a sudden deluge of tears.

"I don't believe it," Hayley said fiercely. "Elliot *loves* you, Mother! I know he loves you!"

"No—" a long, shuddering inhalation "—he doesn't."

"Yes, he does."

Her mother gazed at her with anguished eyes. "Then wh-why is h-he having an af-fair?" she demanded rawly.

"Has he told you he's having an affair?"

Pamela shook her head, her mouth trembling. Tears were running off her chin and spotting the front of her dress.

"Then how do you know?"

"M-Muriel Esterhaus." It came out in a miserable whisper.

"Muriel Esterhaus?" Hayley repeated blankly.

"My fr-friend. The w-woman we...we flew t-to New York with."

The name slotted into place. "The gossip?"

Her mother nodded, pressing the fingers of one hand to her lips.

"Well, how does *she* know?"

"Because... because she saw them t-together." Pamela's throat worked convulsively for several seconds. "She saw Elliot and a...a young blond b-bimbo. At...at l-lunch. Today."

Hayley felt herself go white. Her throat closed up. Elliot.

A young blond bimbo. *Bimbo?*

At lunch.

Today.

Dear Lord, she'd known someone was watching them. She'd known it!

"A mistake," Hayley choked out. She packed all the conviction she could into the assertion. "It must be...a mistake."

Pamela stared at her. In a bizarre way, the expression on her face reminded Hayley of the look young Mikey Ross had worn when he'd read Nick's fake ID.

"Do you... do you really think it c-could be, Hayley?" she asked tremulously after nearly thirty seconds of silence.

"Yes," Hayley answered emphatically, gripping her mother's hands with her own. "Absolutely. Elliot Parker loves you, Mother. I know he does. *You* know he does. Besides, even if he had the bad taste to have an affair with a blond bimbo, do you really think he'd be stupid enough to parade her around in public?"

Her mother blinked several times, then sniffed. "No," she said slowly. "He's a v-very intelligent man."

"He's brilliant, Mother."

Pamela mulled this over, her forehead pleating. "Muriel *is* a little n-nearsighted," she offered tentatively. "She doesn't like to w-wear her glasses."

"In other words, she's as blind as a bat and vain on top of being a nasty-minded gossip," Hayley declared acidly.

"Oh, no. She's not *that* bad," her mother protested. She disengaged her hands from Hayley's, then mopped her cheeks and blew her nose. "She...she has been wrong about things, though. M-Muriel, I mean."

"And she's wrong about this, Mother," Hayley said feelingly. "Trust me. She's totally wrong. Elliot is *not* being unfaithful to you."

"Do you honestly believe that, dear?" Pamela questioned. "You're such a good judge of character."

Somehow, Hayley prevented herself from flinching—or flushing—at the last remark. "Yes, I honestly believe it," she said. "I believe it with all my heart."

It took Hayley nearly an hour to get her mother completely calmed down. The soothing process required a lot of lying, but she didn't think she had any other choice. To tell one truth—aside from the truth about Elliot Parker's feelings—would lead to another and another and another. And that would lead to disaster. It seemed to her that honesty was the worst possible policy at this point.

Ultimately she bundled Pamela into a cab and dispatched her back to her hotel. She then raced back up to her apartment and telephoned Elliot Parker. He was predictably appalled by the latest turn of events. After muttering something about strangling Muriel Esterhaus, he assured Hayley that she'd done the right thing. He then related what Special Agent Oliver had told him and added, without elaborating, that he'd had a very illuminating visit from Nick O'Neill. He concluded with a promise that he would continue to shield Pamela from what was going on as long as he possibly could.

There wasn't much to be said after that. Hayley bade her future stepfather a weary good-night and hung up the phone.

"What next?" she said aloud, trying not to wonder what Nick had said to Elliot and what Elliot had said in return.

"What next" turned out to be a call to Michelle Becker's answering machine. The message was recorded at 10:57 p.m. and lasted twenty-two seconds.

"This is Philippe de Sante. I have need of an escort tomorrow night. I hope we can come to terms. I trust you remember the hotel where I'm staying. I'm in suite 1712. Call me, Michelle. I think you will find the evening rewarding . . . and amusing."

Thirteen

Nick took a step back, steeling himself against the temptations of Hayley's silken skin and provocative perfume. He'd had his hands all over her during the past fifteen minutes, but that had been business. Strictly business.

The kind of "strictly business" that had nearly gotten Special Agent Leahy a fist in the face when he'd suggested that he—not Nick—be the one to go to Hayley's apartment and equip her with a body bug before she went off for her rendezvous with Philippe de Sante.

"How does it feel?" Nick questioned, a hint of raspiness in his voice. He jammed his hands into the pockets of his black leather jacket.

Hayley pivoted, her body tingling from Nick's touch. She knew her cheeks were flushed. Her blood was fizzing like champagne.

"It itches," she complained, plucking at the elegantly draped front of the black velvet gown she was wearing. She met Nick's gaze for a few moments, then glanced downward.

"Good."

Hayley's head snapped up. The baroque pearls dangling from her earlobes swung wildly. *"Good?"*

Nick nodded. "Yeah. It'll keep you from forgetting you've got it on."

"I hardly think I'm going to forget I'm wired for sound!" she snapped.

"It's easy to get caught up in the game, Hayley," he warned her. "Sometimes an itch gives you an edge."

There was a taut silence.

Hayley ran her tongue over her lips, struggling to control her emotions. The job she was facing required a clear head and a cool manner, she reminded herself. In fact, her whole *life* required them!

Nick balled his hands inside his pockets, trying to ignore the sheen of moisture Hayley had left when she'd licked her mouth. He fought to tame the desire that was uncoiling in the pit of his belly. This was not a night he could afford to be distracted.

He sucked in a deep breath through his nose, then expelled it slowly through his mouth. He repeated the procedure two more times, exerting every bit of self-discipline he had. The tension in his groin eased a bit.

"Let's go over the drill," he said finally.

Hayley opened her eyes and gave Nick a sharp look. "We've been over it."

"Let's go over it again."

"I know what I'm supposed to do."

"I don't doubt that," Nick answered, meaning it. "Just remind the people who're tuned in what to listen for."

Hayley smoothed her palm against the skirt of her gown, considering the first part of his response. Did Nick genuinely believe she was capable of handling this situation? she wondered suddenly. He'd vociferously objected when she'd initially volunteered her services as Michelle Becker to Agents Oliver and Leahy. And, although he'd ultimately acquiesced to her involvement, he obviously hadn't been happy about it. Had he changed his mind? Or was he simply trying to bolster her confidence?

"Hayley?" Nick prompted, taking his hands out of his pockets.

She lifted her chin and began to rattle off the instructions that had been drummed into her. "My assignment is to decorate Philippe de Sante's arm and keep track of who he talks to and what he talks about. If he does anything suspicious—if I see him hand off something to someone— I'm supposed to say 'Excuse me, I need to go to the powder room.' Not the bathroom. Not the ladies' lounge. The *powder* room. And once I say 'Excuse me, I need to go to the powder room,' I walk away."

"There are going to be agents there to take de Sante down," Nick reminded her. "Once you say the code phrase, we'll give them the signal to move in. It should be quick and clean. De Sante doesn't carry a gun. He's contemptuous of people who do. But, at the same time, he's never been caught at anything before, so there's no way of predicting what he'll do if he is. You get clear as quickly as you can. Walk away and don't look back."

"Don't look back," Hayley echoed. She lifted her right arm and patted her upswept hair.

"What if de Sante doesn't do anything suspicious?" Nick questioned, unable to stop himself from tracking the sweetly sensual stir of Hayley's breasts beneath the bodice of her gown. The bra she was wearing—the wispy, black lace bra he'd seen when he'd been taping her body bug into place— offered very little in the way of restraint.

"I wait until the end of the evening and then tell him I'm starting to feel sick." She smiled crookedly. "Don't worry. I'll be convincing. I faked my way out of gym all through high school."

Nick grinned briefly, then grew serious. "Don't—under any circumstances—go back to the hotel with him," he said. He'd been prepared to go to the mat on this issue, but he hadn't had to. While the FBI had wanted Hayley, despite her lack of undercover training, to go right to the limit with de Sante, Al Kozlow had rejected the idea the instant it had been proposed.

The intensity of Nick's gaze made Hayley's heart skip a beat. "I know," she said throatily. "I won't."

"If de Sante insists, make a scene."

Hayley gave a nervous laugh, a sudden shiver running through her. "I hope it won't come to that."

"So do I. But you've got to be prepared."

There was another silence. Hayley glanced around, fingering the lush material of her gown. She could feel Nick watching her. "You know what I'm most nervous about?" she finally asked.

"Your mother," Nick answered unhesitatingly. He'd been present when Hayley had returned Philippe de Sante's phone call. He'd seen her expression when she'd realized that the "rewarding and amusing" evening the Frenchman had in mind for Michelle Becker involved attending the gala that had brought her mother and Elliot Parker to New York.

Her gaze slewed to his face. "How did—?"

"I know you, angel," he said simply.

The endearment Hayley had rejected so firmly during the past few days brought a rush of hot blood to her face. She wanted to reject the word and what it implied again, to deny that Nick knew her at all, but she couldn't. She opened her mouth to speak and nothing came out.

"It's going to be all right," Nick told her after several moments. "Elliot's been briefed. He'll take care of your mother." And I'll take care of you, he vowed silently.

"I hope so," she whispered. The words were tremulous.

"Don't be afraid."

She looked at him, her pulse scrambling in response to the tender intensity of his tone. The expression in his hazel eyes made her breath clog in her throat. She knew he was talking about much more than tonight... than this situation.

"It's hard not to be, Nick," she confessed finally.

Slowly Nick reached out and stroked his fingertips against the curve of her face. She quivered at the careful, caressing contact. Her eyes widened, her lips parted. For one heartstopping second, she turned her cheek into his palm.

"I know," he told her softly, then forced himself to withdraw his hand. "Believe me, Hayley. I know."

"Have you ... ever been afraid?"

He nodded. "Oh, yeah."

He didn't kiss her then, but he desperately wanted to.

Hayley saw that he wanted to and desperately wished that he had.

A few minutes later Nick climbed into the back of a panel truck filled with surveillance equipment. There were three other men already in place—Al Kozlow and Special Agents Oliver and Leahy.

"How's the signal?" Nick asked. One of the most difficult things he'd ever done in his life was to accept that he was going to have to play a passive role for most—if not all—of this evening. While there'd been some discussion about the possibility of his going to the gala as Neil James, he'd ultimately conceded that such a move would be out of character. His appearance would be more likely to spook de Sante than to protect Hayley.

"No problem," Special Agent Oliver answered, giving a thumbs-up signal.

"Clear as a bell," Special Agent Leahy confirmed.

"Good," Nick said tersely, reaching for the 9 mm pistol he'd stashed in the truck before going up to Hayley's apartment. He was already wearing the holster for the gun anchored in the small of his back.

"Let's get this show on the road," Al Kozlow ordered.

Nick felt the truck pull into traffic.

"Champagne, ma'am?" the waiter inquired, extending a gleaming silver tray to Hayley.

"Thank you," she answered, taking a glass.

"Champagne, sir?"

Philippe de Sante surveyed the tray for a moment, then shook his head dismissively. The waiter nodded and moved.

Hayley took a tiny sip of the sparkling wine. "You don't like champagne, Philippe?"

"I appreciate good champagne," he returned, reaching into the inner breast pocket of his evening jacket and bringing out his cigarette case and lighter. He didn't so much handle the items as he fondled them.

Hayley held her glass up. "I take it this doesn't meet your standards?"

"Adequate for the occasion," he responded with a very Gallic shrug. "I have a bottle of Cristal waiting for us back in my suite. I trust it will prove adequate for that occasion."

Hayley smiled and controlled an instinctive shiver.

De Sante lit a cigarette. He inhaled deeply, then expelled two narrow streams of smoke through his nostrils. He glanced around. If he was looking for someone—or something—specific, Hayley couldn't tell.

"Pardon me."

The source of this interruption was a painfully thin brunette in a heavily embroidered gown. She was holding an unlit cigarette and regarding Philippe expectantly from beneath arched, over-plucked eyebrows.

"Do you mind?" she asked, bringing the cigarette to her scarlet-painted lips.

"But, of course," Philippe returned, firing his lighter.

"Thanks," the woman said, taking a puff. She gave Hayley a swift up-down look. "I know it's a filthy habit," she commented with an artificial laugh. "But it's either smoking or stuffing my face." She laughed again, then drifted away.

De Sante made a soft, derisive sound and put both his cigarette case and lighter back into his breast pocket.

Hayley took another sip of champagne and looked around. She and her companion—plus several hundred other people—were gathered in the newest wing of one of New York City's great art museums. The cavernous space had been temporarily transformed into a gilded and glittering party palace. A string quartet was playing in one corner of the hall. There were huge arrangements of flowers everywhere. Lavishly stocked buffet tables offered an array of foods designed to please even the most jaded palate.

"You are enjoying yourself?" Philippe inquired after several moments.

Hayley quickly shifted her gaze back to him. As she did so, she caught a glimpse of a hatchet-faced older woman with helmet-smooth cap of black hair. The woman, who was swathed in a singularly unattractive shade of chartreuse, was glaring at her as though she were a cockroach scuttling across a bowl of Beluga caviar.

"Being with you, how could I not?" Hayley countered, shoving the image of the jet-haired woman out of her mind. The only woman she cared about this evening had silvery curls and was wearing a gown of kingfisher blue chiffon. She'd spotted her mother twice so far. Although she didn't think Pamela had seen her, she was pretty certain Elliot had.

De Sante's thin lips curled up at the corners. His heavy eyelids eased down slightly. "Did you play the coquette for my friend, Neil James?"

It was the third—no, the fourth—time he'd brought up Nick's cover name. Hayley was confident she'd finessed the subject fairly skillfully in each previous instance. Now, however, she decided she needed to demonstrate that while Michelle Becker more or less made her living by lying down, she wasn't a doormat.

"What I did with your friend, Neil, is none of your concern, Philippe," she said coolly. "Just as what I do with you is none of his."

Down in the surveillance truck, Special Agent Leahy sucked in his breath at this remark, obviously deeming it unwise. "Jeez—"

"No," Nick said swiftly. He'd experienced a strange pang when he'd heard the tone Hayley had used to put down de Sante. Even with the inevitable overlay of crowd noise and electronic static, it had been pure Ice Princess. "She's playing it just right. Michelle Becker isn't supposed to be a walkover. Besides, discretion is key to her business. Call girls can't kiss and tell."

Hayley saw Philippe's eyes narrow and had the feeling he was reevaluating her. "In other words, you do not—what is the phrase?—'kiss and tell?'" he inquired silkenly.

Hayley took another small sip of champagne and let her gaze wander. She wondered which of the people she was seeing were government agents. Out of the corner of her eye, she noticed that the woman in the vile yellow-green dress was still watching her.

"Sometimes I kiss and there's nothing to tell," she replied with a delicate shrug. "Other times I don't kiss and there's everything to tell."

"But you don't." De Sante inhaled another lungful of cigarette smoke, then breathed it out.

Hayley shook her head, her pearl drop earrings bobbing against her cheeks.

"Never?"

She gave her companion an up-from-under her lashes look. "I never say never."

"But you *are* discreet."

"Among a great many other things."

De Sante smiled thinly. "I can imagine."

Hayley smiled back, experiencing an odd rush of exhilaration. I know something you don't know, she thought. "Somehow, I doubt that."

Nick tensed, hearing an undercurrent of mockery in Hayley's voice.

"Careful, angel," he warned softly. He knew how strong the temptation to score points off a mark could be. He also knew what a dangerous mistake it could be to succumb to that temptation.

"Indeed?" de Sante countered, lifting a brow.

Hayley shifted, suddenly conscious of the wire she was wearing. Watch it, she thought, remembering what Nick had told her earlier. Don't get caught up in the game. "A woman likes to feel she has some secrets," she responded.

The Frenchman studied her for a few seconds, then nodded slowly. "Of course," he concurred. "Still, I am curious about Monsieur James."

* * *

"Well, he's curious about you, too," Nick muttered.

"You really made some impression on this bastard, O'Neill," Agent Oliver commented.

"He makes an impression on everybody he meets," Kozlow responded. "Just not necessarily the right one."

"I'm sure Neil James is curious about you, too, Philippe," Hayley parried. "But other people's curiosity is the one thing I make a point of leaving unsatisfied."

"Mmm." De Sante was looking around once again. He suddenly seemed to focus on something.

The skin on the back of Hayley's neck prickled. Turning her head, she followed the line of his gaze. Her fingers tightened convulsively on the stem of her champagne glass when she realized what had captured his attention.

Her mother and Elliot Parker were standing with a small cluster of people no more than fifteen feet away. While Pamela had her back turned, Elliot was looking right at her. Their eyes met for an instance, then he averted his gaze.

Hayley heard Philippe de Sante chuckle. It was not a pleasant sound. "I believe I mentioned you might find this evening an amusing one, Michelle," he observed.

Hayley looked at him, willing herself to appear indifferent to Elliot's presence. "Do you enjoy seeing other men squirm?" she queried.

"Oh, yes. Very much."

"What the hell does that mean?" Leahy demanded, frowning.

"I think it has something to do with Elliot Parker," Nick answered.

"The guy seemed very together when I briefed him," Oliver commented approvingly. "He'll stay cool."

"Let's just hope Jerome's mother does the same," Kozlow said.

De Sante signaled a passing waiter. The man approached, carrying a tray laden with empty glasses and dirty plates. Hayley placed her champagne flute on it. The Frenchman stubbed out his cigarette on one of the plates, then sent the server on his way.

"Has the Congressman been enjoying your services for long?" he inquired, reaching into his breast pocket once more.

Hayley willed herself not to look toward Elliot and her mother. Feigning a pout, she lifted one hand and stroked her fingertips lightly against de Sante's arm.

"First Neil. Now Elliot," she murmured. "Do you *really* want to spend the evening asking me about other men, Philippe? I'd much prefer to talk about you."

De Sante smiled, taking out his case and lighter. "Would you?" he countered. He selected a cigarette, lit it, then returned the case and lighter to his jacket.

"Absolutely," Hayley purred. Michelle Becker got paid to pander, that's what she'd do. "I've always found it infinitely more interesting to concentrate on the man of the moment than the men of the past."

De Sante blew out a stream of smoke. "No doubt you've found it more rewarding as well," he responded knowingly.

"Oh, that, too," Hayley agreed, deciding that Michelle Becker wouldn't cavil at a reference to the profitability of her profession.

"Perhaps you will—"

"Excuse me, please. But could you possibly supply me with a match?"

The source of this interruption was a short man with slicked-back black hair, a thin mustache, and skin the color and texture of cordovan leather. He was holding an unlit cigarillo between his thumb and forefinger.

Leahy rolled his eyes in disgust. "Is de Sante on retainer from the tobacco companies or something?"

"Assuredly," Philippe told the short man, reaching into his jacket.

Hayley darted a quick glance at Elliot and her mother. She stiffened as she realized that her mother was starting to turn in her direction. Quickly, she shifted her position and focused her gaze back on Philippe and the would-be smoker.

Please, she prayed silently, forcing herself to smile. Her heart was racing. Her stomach was roiling. Please, don't let her see me.

"Thank you," the short man said, leaning in to accept a light from the match de Sante had just struck. He sucked on the cigarillo, making its tip glow a bright orange, then exhaled a plume of smoke.

"My pleasure," Philippe replied. "Would you like to keep—?" He offered the book of matches he was holding.

"Yes. I would appreciate it," the short man answered. He took the matchbook and thrust it into his pants pocket. "Again, my thanks."

"Again, my pleasure."

The short man turned and walked away.

"Something stinks," Nick stated.

"Stinks?" Leahy repeated blankly.

"What?" Oliver asked at the same time.

Nick got out of his seat. "I think de Sante just gave his lighter to some guy who asked for a match. His *gold* lighter."

"Bingo," Kozlow said.

"Are you all right, *cheri?*"

"Oh, yes, fine," Hayley answered a bit breathlessly. The matchbook that had just exchanged hands had been something of a shock to her. The cover had been embossed with the name of a restaurant. The *same* restaurant where she and Elliot Parker had encountered Philippe de Sante the day before. Seeing it had made her—

Wait a moment.

A matchbook?

Why in heaven's name would Philippe de Sante be carrying around a matchbook?

Unless—

"Michelle?" de Sante questioned.

Hayley moistened her lips with a quick lick of her tongue. "Will you excuse me for a few moments, Philippe?" she asked, fighting the urge to overenunciate the words. "I need to go to the powder room."

"That's it!" Nick declared, grabbing the handle that released the truck's side door. "We take down de Sante and the guy whose cigarette he just lit."

Hayley never learned exactly what triggered the mayhem that followed. The official report on that part of the operation was rather vague, and press accounts based on eyewitness statements were wildly contradictory.

Following Nick's instructions, she turned and began to walk away from Philippe de Sante almost before she finished excusing herself. She took three steps, then veered off realizing she was heading toward her mother and Elliot. Three more steps and she realized she was on a collision course with the black-haired woman in the bile-colored dress. She shifted direction again, moving as quickly as she could without calling attention to herself.

And then, without warning—

"Look out! A gun! He has a gun!" someone cried.

Hayley whirled, just in time to see a man in an evening jacket who *wasn't* Philippe de Sante being tackled from behind by a uniformed security guard who'd materialized out of nowhere. The man went down on the floor with a thud. In the same instant another man in a waiter's outfit grabbed the guard and shouted something about being with the U.S. government.

People started shouting. Shoving. She even saw one woman swoon.

And Philippe de Sante was very calmly heading toward an exit.

Hayley did what she knew Nick would do. She followed her instincts and went after the snake.

"De Sante is heading for the far south exit," she said distinctly, trusting that someone was still listening to her. "The other man we want is short, very tanned, and ha dark, slicked-back hair and a thin mustache. There's a matchbook in his left pants pocket. A matchbook from—'' she named the restaurant. ''I think that's what we're looking for.''

She paused only once in her pursuit of Philippe de Sante and that was to snatch up something she thought she could use as a weapon. She hoped it would prove adequate to the occasion.

It was chaos.

Cursing under his breath, Nick ruthlessly elbowed a path through the mob of socialites fighting to get out of the museum hall. He scanned the well-dressed horde, searching...searching...

Where the hell was—

There!

''Move it! Move it, dammit!'' Nick yelled, battling his way through the surging throng.

Maybe de Sante heard his voice. Maybe he didn't. Nick never found out. Whatever the case, his quarry suddenly stopped moving and turned. His gaze met Nick's. His eyes widened as he took in Nick's street tough attire.

Nick saw the instant in which de Sante realized that he must have been played for a fool. The realization sparked no fear, just fury.

Nick reached for the gun in the small of his back.

De Sante's face contorted. He reached into his breast pocket.

And then Nick saw Hayley. He felt his heart stop as she emerged from the roiling crowd like an avenging angel, brandishing an unopened bottle of champagne. Her intention was horrifyingly clear.

''Freeze, de Sante! This is the FBI!'' Special Agent Leahy suddenly bellowed from somewhere to the Frenchman's left.

De Sante withdrew his hand from inside his jacket. He was holding his cigarette lighter. His thin lips twisted into a smile. He twitched his thumb against the lighter and—

Ku-thunk!

Hayley swung the champagne bottle, two-handed, like a tennis racket, clobbering him squarely between the shoulder blades.

De Sante staggered forward, his eyes bulging. The cigarette lighter went flying out of his hands. It hit the floor and exploded in a cloud of white gas.

More screams. Lots and lots of them.

Nick sprang like a tiger, tackling de Sante low and bringing him down hard.

He admitted to himself later that he would have relished a fight, but the Frenchman had none left in him. In point of fact, Philippe de Sante had been knocked unconscious.

"*Nick*. Oh...God...Nick!" The voice was Hayley's. She sounded all choked up.

Nick levered himself off de Sante's limp body, his nostrils twitching, his eyes starting to sting. One small corner of his brain identified the acrid odor of the gas that had exploded out of de Sante's lighter.

It was Mace. Not some diabolical nerve agent. Not some deadly biologic weapon. It was plain, ordinary, protect-yourself-from-muggers Mace.

Nick looked up at Hayley. There were tears streaming down her cheeks. She was clutching the champagne bottle to her chest, and she was staring down at him with her heart in her eyes.

He opened his mouth to say something to her. Something he'd said before and she'd refused to accept. The expression on her face suggested she might finally be ready to take to heart.

But it had to wait. At that moment, a shot rang out.

A woman shrieked.

If there were degrees of chaos, Nick decided grimly, this was one of the worst.

The shot came from the other end of the hall. Once the still-unconscious Philippe de Sante had been consigned to the custody of a teary-eyed Agent Leahy, that's where Hayley and Nick headed.

Hayley was in no way prepared for what they found.

The man who'd accepted the restaurant matchbook was being dragged away in handcuffs by Special Agent Oliver and a man in a tuxedo. The suspect was demanding the services of an attorney.

Elliot Parker was lying on the floor clutching his left shoulder. Blood was seeping out between his fingers.

His soon-to-be wife was kneeling beside him, weeping. She was also pleading to be forgiven for having doubted his fidelity.

"Oh...Elliot. *Elliot.*" Pamela Delaney Jerome Martinez de la Madrid Touissante Pynchley-Smythe Horowitz sobbed. "I'm sorry, darling. I'm sorry I ever thought you were ch-cheating on me!"

"Dear Lord!" Hayley gasped, elbowing her way through the throng of people surrounding the scene. She, too, knelt down on the floor. "What happened?"

Her mother looked at her, blue eyes awash with tears. "Elliot saved my l-life," she said brokenly. "That horrible short man had a gun and he grabbed me. He...he was going to kill m-me! But Elliot jumped him and rescued me, except...except he got sh-shot—"

"Now, now, Pamela," Elliot protested, struggling to sit up. "It's only a flesh wound."

"Take it easy, Congressman," Nick ordered firmly, hunkering down next to the injured man. He began to undo the buttons of Elliot's dress shirt.

"M-Michael?" Pamela asked, gazing at him in astonishment. "What are you doing—"

"You little tramp!" a feminine voice suddenly shrilled.

Stunned, Hayley looked up and saw the hatchet-faced brunette she'd noticed earlier bearing down on her like a heat-seeking missile.

"You get away from him, you hussy!" the woman demanded.

"M-M-Muriel?" Pamela stammered.

Oh, no, Hayley thought. No. Not *Muriel Esterhaus!*

"It's her, Pamela," the brunette declared wrathfully. "It's the blond bimbo I saw with Elliot!"

This is the end, Hayley told herself, wishing there was a hole in the floor so she could crawl into it. This is the absolute and utter end.

"Look, lady—" Nick started angrily, glancing up from Elliot's wound. The former congressman had been right in his assessment. It was not a very serious injury.

Hayley saw her mother's eyes flash with indignation. "My daughter is *not* a bimbo, Muriel Esterhaus!"

The other woman tuned puce. "Your daughter?" she shrieked, staggering backward, clutching her chartreuse-covered bosom. "Oh, God! It's even worse than I—oh, God! It's *incest!*"

The gathered crowd gave a collective gasp.

"No, ma'am," the gravelly voice of Al Kozlow contradicted flatly. "It's national security."

Hayley looked up at her boss. He was standing about a yard away, smiling like a well-fed Cheshire cat. In his right hand, he held a matchbook.

Fourteen

———

"It's all my fault," Pamela declared with a heavy sigh.

"*Your* fault?" Hayley echoed, stunned. "Mother, weren't you listening? I *lied* to you! I lied to you over and over!"

Hayley and her mother were sitting in a hospital lounge waiting for the definitive medical assessment of Elliot's injuries. They'd arrived at the hospital roughly two hours before. Hayley had spent a few minutes of that two hours in a ladies' room, pulling off the surveillance wire she'd been wearing. She'd spent most of the rest of it confessing to her mother. While she wasn't sure what kind of reaction she'd expected her confession to evoke, she was positive it wasn't the one she was getting.

"I've been terribly selfish all these years," Pamela stated. "I've depended on you too much. Even when you were a little girl, I expected you to be the organized and responsible one in the family while I just went on my merry way. And the worst thing is, I never tried to explain to you why I behaved the way I did. I just expected you to cope and keep up. And you did, Hayley. You always d-did." She paused for a moment, her throat working. "I owe you the truth, dear. The truth about me. And the truth about your father.''

"I don't understand," Hayley said uneasily after several seconds.

"Your father was not exactly the man I've made him out to be, dear."

"He . . . wasn't?"

"I've always told you what a stable, dependable man he was. And he was. He always did the right thing, although not always in the conventional way. But there were times when he was . . . was . . ." Pamela paused, blushing, then finally concluded, ". . . a bit of a rogue."

"Daddy?"

"Oh, I don't mean anything bad by it," Pamela assured her quickly. "Quite the contrary. It's just that life with your father was . . . unpredictable. He could be very spontaneous. We, ah, used to—ahem—pretend to be other people. We'd . . . make up, ah, fantasies and, well, play them out."

Hayley felt her own cheeks heat. Her mother and father—pretending to be other people? *Playing out fantasies?*

"Oh, dear," Pamela said in a distressed voice. "I've shocked you."

"No," Hayley disagreed. "Not . . . shocked. Surprised." And she was the person who hated surprises. But there was something about this one . . .

"Your father was everything I ever wanted in a man, Hayley," her mother went on. "When he died . . . I felt so empty. So incomplete. I thought that going new places and doing new things would help fill the void. And it did for a little while. But the emptiness always came back. And as for the other men I married—well, each one of them let me recapture a piece of Henry. His strength. His humor. His romantic nature. But after a while I'd always realize that a piece wasn't enough after I'd had the whole."

There was a long silence.

"I wish you'd told me before," Hayley finally said blinking against a sudden pricking of tears.

"I should have," her mother responded. "I know I should have. I just hope I haven't left it too late for you and Nick."

"For... for me and Nick?"

Her mother nodded, then commented casually, "I like the name Nick O'Neill better than Michael Becker, you know. Even though they're the same man."

"Wh-what?"

"They're the same man," Pamela repeated. "Think about it, Hayley. Was the Michael Becker you created some pin-striped paragon of predictability? No! He was a man who went winging off to Tierra del Fuego at the drop of a hat. A man who swept you off your feet and kept you on your toes. You may have told yourself you were trying to appeal to me when you made up Michael Becker, but you were drawing on your own dreams. And as for the man I met Wednesday night—" Pamela smiled crookedly "—well, he's everything you said he was and more."

Hayley realized she'd begun trembling. Was it possible?

"Dear, all I've ever wanted was for you to have a chance to be as happy with someone as I was with Henry," Pamela went on fervently. "As happy as my heart tells me I'm going to be with Elliot. Please—*please,* don't close yourself off. Don't be afraid."

"It's hard not to be," Hayley said after several taut seconds.

"But you *do* love him, don't you? Nick, I mean."

Hayley looked down. "Yes," she whispered, a peculiar quiver running through her. She wondered where Nick was. He'd had to remain at the museum while she and her mother had gone to the hospital with Elliot.

"Have you told him?" The question was very gentle.

"I told him... I didn't want to love him and I didn't want him to love me." She took a deep breath, then admitted, "But that's not the truth."

"What is the truth then, angel?" a resonant male voice asked.

Hayley's head came up. She turned.

Nick was standing a few feet away, legs braced apart, hands fisted at his sides. He was dressed very much the way he'd been dressed the first time she'd seen him. But his expression—oh, sweet heaven, his expression!

Hayley got up from her seat very slowly. She moved to Nick with the same deliberate pace. Staring into his compelling face, she brought her hands up and pressed them flat against his chest. She felt him stiffen at the contact. She saw his hazel eyes spark emerald and gold.

"This," she said huskily, "is the truth."

And then she rose up on her toes, slid her hands up to lock around his neck, and kissed him full on the mouth with all the love in her soul.

Nick's arms went around her. He kissed her back with hot, hungry passion. She felt one of his hands glide up her back to tangle in her hair. The other stroked down to curve against her bottom, urging her closer.

"Nick..." She shifted against him, trying to get closer still.

He groaned her name, his tongue delving deep into her mouth.

They were both trembling with need when the kiss finally came to an end. Nick's breath was coming in ragged pants. His eyes were blazing. A flush of sexual excitement rode high on the hard lines of his cheekbones.

"I love you," Hayley told him throatily.

"I love you, too," he answered, his voice even thicker than hers.

"I knew it," Pamela announced with a sentimental sigh.

Hayley stiffened. After a moment she turned to face her mother. She felt as though her entire body was blushing. She didn't know what to say.

Nick, it seemed, did. "I just saw your fiancé," he announced.

Pamela lit up like a Broadway marquee. "You did? Is he going to be all right?"

"Good as new, according to the doctors. He should be here in a minute or two. They wanted him to stay in the hospital overnight, but he said no."

Hayley's mother rose to her feet. "That's probably because he knows how much I love to play nurse," she com mented happily, fluffing her silvery curls. Then, suddenly, she cocked her head and gazed at Nick assessingly.

Hayley shifted, not quite trusting the gleam she saw in her mother's eyes. She felt the reassuring stroke of Nick's hand.

"Hayley's told me everything," Pamela said. "But I'd like to make absolutely certain I know your real name and exactly who you are."

"My real name is Nicholas James O'Neill," came the steady reply. "And I'm the man who's going to marry your daughter—if she'll have me."

"Has anyone ever told you you're impossible?"

"Just you, angel."

Hayley lifted her arms in a long, languid stretch. "In other words, I'm the only one you haven't been able to con, hmm?"

"I wouldn't even try," Nick promised her, watching the provocative movement of her breasts beneath the black velvet of her gown. Although his tone was teasing, his intention was true.

Hayley began combing her fingers through her hair, deliciously aware of his scrutiny. They were in the living room of her apartment. They'd adjourned there after seeing her mother and Elliot off from the hospital. The cab ride to her building had been made in emotionally-charged silence. This wasn't because everything that needed to be said had been said. It was because what needed to be said had to be said in private.

"So..." she began, then paused to clear her throat.

"So?" Nick prompted softly after a few moments.

"So, you're the man who's going to marry me."

"*If* you'll have me."

"And if I won't?"

Nick spread his hands. "I won't marry anybody."

"Oh." It was little more than an exhalation. "Well..."

"Yes?"

She moistened her lips, her gaze flicking toward her bedroom then back to Nick's face. "I seem to remember—ahem—having had you, Nick."

He lifted a brow. "One night."

"Three times." A voluptuous shiver ran through her.

"Want to go for four?"

"In one night?"

His smile was very male. "If the spirit's willing . . ."

Hayley knew how the adage ended. She also knew that her flesh was anything but weak at this moment. Except for her knees. They were going to give way in another few seconds.

Her gaze slid down from Nick's face. Down his throat, down his chest, down lower still.

While his flesh was pretty well covered up, there were no indications of any weakness. In fact, the potent bulge below his belt buckle seemed to suggest—

"Hayley?" Nick questioned a little hoarsely.

She lifted her gaze. "I'll have you, Nicholas James O'Neill," she told him with tender solemnity. "For the rest of my life, I'll have you."

"Did I do this?" Nick asked, feathering his fingers over a reddened mark he'd just discovered on Hayley's skin.

"I . . . I had some—mmm—trouble with the tape you used on the wire." Hayley closed her eyes, quivering in response to his caressing touch.

He dipped his head and pressed his lips against the abrasion. Hayley caught her breath sharply as she felt the delicate lap of his tongue.

"Better?" he asked.

She opened her eyes and smiled at him. "Much."

They were standing a foot or two from Hayley's bed, trying to undress each other between kisses and caresses. Nick was down to his jeans. Hayley was wearing nothing but underwear, stockings, and one baroque pearl earring.

Nick's hands moved to her breasts. He cupped them lovingly, tantalizing the peaking tips through the fragile fabric of her black lace bra. Hayley arched, her head tilting back, as he flicked the sensitive buds of flesh with his thumbnails.

"Oh, N-Nick," she moaned, feeling herself catch fire.

He undid the clasp with a deft twist of his fingers. A moment later the flimsy bit of lingerie joined her black velvet gown on the floor.

"Lovely," he declared in a low, liquid voice. "Perfect."

Hayley ran her hands over his naked torso, fingers splayed, relishing the responsive tightening of his supple muscles. She savored the springy crispness of his chest hair, then turned her attention to his nipples. She teased the tightly furled buttons until Nick made a sound deep in his throat.

They kissed again. He seduced her tongue with his own, sampling the sweetness that was more addictive than any drug. His hunger increased heartbeat by heartbeat. The fluid shift of her body against his was almost more than he could endure.

"I want you, Nick," Hayley whispered, underscoring her desire with nipping kisses and quick, hot licks. "I need you. I need you . . . so much. I want to touch you. All of you."

Her hands were shaking as she began to undo his belt, but she eventually accomplished her objective.

The pop of a snap.

The metallic rasp of a zipper.

"Dear . . . *Hayley*," Nick groaned as her fingers found him, enfolded him. The caress was the epitome of intimacy and it brought him to the brink of explosion. "Too much."

A few seconds later they were both completely naked.

A few seconds after that, they were on her bed, locked in each other's arms.

"Angel . . . my angel . . ." Nick whispered hotly, raining kisses on her face, her throat, her breasts. He wooed her . . . wantoned her . . . made her writhe and cry out.

Hayley stroked him. Languidly at first, then with increasing urgency. She twisted wildly as one of his hands slipped down her body and between her thighs. She felt his fingers trace the hidden cleft of her womanhood, then ease inside to stoke the secret fire that burned within her.

"Nick . . . please. Oh—*oh!*"

He shifted up and moved over, sliding deep into Hayley's body. She gave herself to him completely, arching up to accept the powerful thrust, welcoming him with soft, shuddering cries. If he had had any chance of delaying the inevitable, he lost it when he felt the first convulsive ripple that signaled her release.

He surrendered to her.

She surrendered to him.

Everything was obliterated...but nothing was destroyed.

"Nick."

"Hmm?"

"What do you think about our working together... undercover?"

"No way."

Hayley lifted her head and gazed at him, wondering if she should be insulted. She hoped not. She seriously doubted she had the energy. "You don't think I did a good job with de Sante?"

Nick ran his hand soothingly down the line of her back. "I think you did a fantastic job. Al thinks you did a fantastic job. Special Agents Oliver and Leahy think you did a fantastic job. Thanks to you, we're not going to have blackmailing terrorists putting the hammerlock on several very senior members of the current administration."

"Is that what—?" Hayley suddenly recalled de Sante's reply to her inquiry about whether he enjoyed watching men squirm.

"There were two microdots on the matchbook. I don't have any details. The FBI technician took a look at the first one and decided we were in highly classified territory. I figure we should watch CNN for announcements of resignations."

Hayley took a moment to absorb this, then returned to her original subject. "If I did such a fantastic job, why are you against us working together undercover?"

"Because—" Nick dropped a kiss on her brow "—we're going to be too famous to go undercover."

"*What?*" She levered herself up.

Nick chuckled wryly. "You mean you didn't notice all those photographers snapping our pictures? Hayley, love, what happened at the museum is going to be front page news all over the country. You have to be anonymous to work undercover."

Hayley stared at him, appalled. "But undercover is what you do, Nick!"

"Not anymore," he answered cheerfully. "I guess it's time to dust off my law degree."

"You...have...a *law*...degree?"

"Surprised?"

"Nick!"

He chuckled again, thoroughly enjoying both Hayley's astonishment and the sight of her naked, rosy-tipped breasts. "Yes, angel," he affirmed. "I have a law degree. I've even passed the New York Bar exam. Of course, I haven't practiced. But I'm sure the Justice Department won't hold that against me."

Hayley shook her head. "Maybe you can pull some strings and get assigned to the team that prosecutes de Sante," she suggested with a trace of sarcasm.

"Maybe," he agreed.

There was a brief silence. Hayley used it to bid a blithe farewell to her neatly organized existence.

"Is there anything else you haven't told me?" she eventually asked.

Nick pondered this for a few seconds, then gave her a smile that made her entire body sizzle. "Only that I realized you were the woman for me the night I took off your clothes and discovered you were wearing red-hot satin underwear."

Six weeks later, on their wedding night, Nicholas James O'Neill took off Hayley Jerome O'Neill's clothes once again and discovered the same thing.

* * * * *

SILHOUETTE®
OFFICIAL SWEEPSTAKES
RULES

NO PURCHASE NECESSARY

1. To enter, complete an Official Entry Form or 3"× 5" index card by hand-printing, in plain block letters, your complete name, address, phone number and age, and mailing it to: Silhouette Fashion A Whole New You Sweepstakes, P.O. Box 9056, Buffalo, NY 14269-9056.

   No responsibility is assumed for lost, late or misdirected mail. Entries must be sent separately with first class postage affixed, and be received no later than December 31, 1991 for eligibility.

2. Winners will be selected by D.L. Blair, Inc., an independent judging organization whose decisions are final, in random drawings to be held on January 30, 1992 in Blair, NE at 10:00 a.m. from among all eligible entries received.

3. The prizes to be awarded and their approximate retail values are as follows: Grand Prize — A brand-new Ford Explorer 4×4 plus a trip for two (2) to Hawaii, including round-trip air transportation, six (6) nights hotel accommodation, a $1,400 meal/spending money stipend and $2,000 cash toward a new fashion wardrobe (approximate value: $28,000) or $15,000 cash; two (2) Second Prizes — A trip to Hawaii, including round-trip air transportation, six (6) nights hotel accommodation, a $1,400 meal/spending money stipend and $2,000 cash toward a new fashion wardrobe (approximate value: $11,000) or $5,000 cash; three (3) Third Prizes — $2,000 cash toward a new fashion wardrobe. All prizes are valued in U.S. currency. Travel award air transportation is from the commercial airport nearest winner's home. Travel is subject to space and accommodation availability, and must be completed by June 30, 1993. Sweepstakes offer is open to residents of the U.S. and Canada who are 21 years of age or older as of December 31, 1991, except residents of Puerto Rico, employees and immediate family members of Torstar Corp., its affiliates, subsidiaries, and all agencies, entities and persons connected with the use, marketing, or conduct of this sweepstakes. All federal, state, provincial, municipal and local laws apply. Offer void wherever prohibited by law. Taxes and/or duties, applicable registration and licensing fees, are the sole responsibility of the winners. Any litigation within the province of Quebec respecting the conduct and awarding of a prize may be submitted to the Régie des loteries et courses du Québec. All prizes will be awarded; winners will be notified by mail. No substitution of prizes is permitted.

4. Potential winners must sign and return any required Affidavit of Eligibility/Release of Liability within 30 days of notification. In the event of noncompliance within this time period, the prize may be awarded to an alternate winner. Any prize or prize notification returned as undeliverable may result in the awarding of that prize to an alternate winner. By acceptance of their prize, winners consent to use of their names, photographs or their likenesses for purposes of advertising, trade and promotion on behalf of Torstar Corp. without further compensation. Canadian winners must correctly answer a time-limited arithmetical question in order to be awarded a prize.

5. For a list of winners (available after 3/31/92), send a separate stamped, self-addressed envelope to: Silhouette Fashion A Whole New You Sweepstakes, P.O. Box 4665, Blair, NE 68009.

PREMIUM OFFER TERMS

To receive your gift, complete the Offer Certificate according to directions. Be certain to enclose the required number of "Fashion A Whole New You" proofs of product purchase (which are found on the last page of every specially marked "Fashion A Whole New You" Silhouette or Harlequin romance novel). Requests must be received no later than December 31, 1991. Limit: four (4) gifts per name, family, group, organization or address. Items depicted are for illustrative purposes only and may not be exactly as shown. Please allow 6 to 8 weeks for receipt of order. Offer good while quantities of gifts last. In the event an ordered gift is no longer available, you will receive a free, previously unpublished Silhouette or Harlequin book for every proof of purchase you have submitted with your request, plus a refund of the postage and handling charge you have included. Offer good in the U.S. and Canada only.   SLFW-SWPR

SILHOUETTE® OFFICIAL SWEEPSTAKES ENTRY FORM

4-FWSDS-4

Complete and return this Entry Form immediately – the more entries you submit, the better your chances of winning!

- Entries must be received by **December 31, 1991.**
- A Random draw will take place on **January 30, 1992.**
- No purchase necessary.

Yes, I want to win a FASHION A WHOLE NEW YOU Sensuous and Adventurous prize from Silhouette:

Name _____ Telephone _____ Age _____

Address _____

City _____ State _____ Zip _____

Return Entries to: Silhouette **FASHION A WHOLE NEW YOU,**
P.O. Box 9056, Buffalo, NY 14269-9056   © 1991 Harlequin Enterprises Limited

PREMIUM OFFER

To receive your free gift, send us the required number of proofs-of-purchase from any specially marked FASHION A WHOLE NEW YOU Silhouette or Harlequin Book with the Offer Certificate properly completed, plus a check or money order (do not send cash) to cover postage and handling payable to Silhouette FASHION A WHOLE NEW YOU Offer. We will send you the specified gift.

OFFER CERTIFICATE

Item	A. SENSUAL DESIGNER VANITY BOX COLLECTION (set of 4) (Suggested Retail Price $60.00)	B. ADVENTUROUS TRAVEL COSMETIC CASE SET (set of 3) (Suggested Retail Price $25.00)
# of proofs-of-purchase	18	12
Postage and Handling	$3.50	$2.95
Check one	☐	☐

Name _____

Address _____

City _____ State _____ Zip _____

Mail this certificate, designated number of proofs-of-purchase and check or money order for postage and handling to: Silhouette **FASHION A WHOLE NEW YOU** Gift Offer, P.O. Box 9057, Buffalo, NY 14269-9057. Requests must be received by December 31, 1991.

ONE PROOF-OF-PURCHASE

4-FWSDP-4

To collect your fabulous free gift you must include the necessary number of proofs-of-purchase with a properly completed Offer Certificate.

© 1991 Harlequin Enterprises Limited

See previous page for details.